AN ISLAND'S TRADE

Nineteenth-Century Shipbuilding on Long Island

AN ISLAND'S TRADE
Nineteenth-Century Shipbuilding on Long Island

by Richard F. Welch

Mystic Seaport Museum
Mystic, Connecticut
1993

Cataloging-in-Publication Data:
Welch, Richard F. (Richard Floyd), 1945-
    An island's trade : nineteenth-century shipbuilding
on Long Island / by Richard F. Welch. – 1st ed. –
Mystic, Conn. : Mystic Seaport Museum, 1993.
    p. : ill., 1 geneal. table, 3 maps, ports. ;   cm.
    Bibliography: p.
    Includes index.

    1. Shipbuilding __ New York (State) __ Long Island.
2. Long Island (N.Y.) __ History. I. Title.

VM24.N7W44

Published by Mystic Seaport Museum, Inc.
75 Greenmanville Avenue
Mystic, CT 06355

THIS BOOK IS DEDICATED
to the memory of
Arthur R. Illing (1883-1963),
who would have known the old shipyards in their decline
and who first taught me
that Long Island has a history,
and to the future of
Kate and Jack,
who will only know of wooden ships
and shipbuilding through books like this.

RFW

Table of Contents

Introduction

The waterfront villages on the North Shore of Long Island are among the most attractive in the Northeast. The deep, glacially cut harbors are scenic in their own right, and much of the local architecture is not yet compromised, modernized or totally destroyed even though highways, strip developments and many thousands of new houses have radically changed the North Shore in this century. While weakened by the blurring effects of suburbanization, community identity and pride survive. Yet few who now walk, work, or play on the streets of these villages are aware that the waterfront, the adjoining streets, and much of the population, were once part of the walking, working and playing of an enterprise far removed from the gourmet foodshops, boutiques, antiques-and-collectibles stores, restaurants and singles bars which dominate so much of village activity in the late twentieth century. Less than a hundred years have passed since the economic, social, and occasionally the political life of these North Shore villages—especially Northport, Setauket, Port Jefferson and Greenport—was dominated by local practitioners of a great national industry—wooden shipbuilding.

Wooden shipbuilding was a perfect example of a pre-industrial-revolution industry. Little start-up capital was required, skills and techniques were passed along by a workshop tradition, simple tools sufficed, and people or animals provided the requisite energy. By the time Long Island took up the trade, more than four hundred years of continually improving techniques and designs had made European ships the most advanced in the world. They were the engine of Europe's exploration and colonization, and it is not surprising that colonists in British North America, ship-dependent from the beginning, soon built their own. North America proved wonderfully suitable for wooden shipbuilding. The deeply indented coastline, abundant lumber from the seemingly endless forests, and an always growing demand for ships, all combined finally to make British North America, and later the United States, the world leader in the production of wooden ships.

Although the great centers of this essential industry were the large cities of New York, Boston and Philadelphia, many peripheral areas played their part. Long Island, especially the villages on the North Shore of Suffolk County, actively pursued the industry to the benefit of local residents and the rising national economy. The deep, protected harbors and bays provided ideal sites for ship construction, while a proximity to the main domestic and international trade routes proved an additional incentive. Lastly, proximity to New York City

A street with a ship at the end – Jones Street, Port Jefferson, circa 1900.

afforded access to supplies, markets for vessels and financial support.

Despite the shadowy and often-romantic conception we have of it, wooden shipbuilding in the big cities and on Long Island has much to tell our own time. At the very least it illustrates the vast national, or at least sectional, scope of one of the nation's most important antebellum industries. It gives evidence of a powerful, widespread capitalistic spirit which inspired a large number of men to grasp at the opportunities offered by shipbuilding. The vessels they built ranged from fishing boats to trading ships that took Long Island craftsmanship to far corners of the world. Perhaps more basically, the history of wooden ship-building on Long Island helps delineate the nature, potentialities and limitations of social and economic life in provincial America during the nineteenth century.

The men who rose to prominence as leaders of the Long Island shipbuild-ing industry were in many ways typical of their time and place—Protestant, native-born, hard-working, respectable in their daily lives and backgrounds. They were successful at their trade, and some succeeded in establishing not only themselves but their families as locally significant, dynamic forces for two or three generations. Not surprisingly, their economic success translated into social and sometimes political leadership as well. Several of them seem possessed of a near-religious belief in the benefits of development, an essential component of the last century's gospel of progress. It is no surprise to see them involved in diversifying their interests and actively encouraging railroad development or the founding of banks. Against these stories of triumphant smalltown capitalism

John R. Mather shipyard crew, 1885, with the planked-up hull of the schooner J.H. Parker.

must be set the stories of those who did not succeed. Why people of the same background, and occasionally the same family, failed to establish permanent, prosperous shipyards is one of the great unknowables of this history.

This record of Long Island's wooden shipbuilding is not solely the story of its provincial entrepreneurs. Examined closely, it reveals much about the lives of working men during the nineteenth century. To the extent that the wooden shipbuilding of the last century survives in popular memory, it usually conjures up images of graceful, tall-masted vessels with clouds of sail, of launching days with flags flying, and quaintly dressed rustics scampering over half-built ships outside a Currier-and-Ives village. Shipyard workers found the reality considerably less romantic. Working hours were long, weeks ran six days, job security was nil, and the possibility of wage increases was virtually non-existent, especially after 1865.

Long Island's wooden shipbuilding rose and fell—as did the nation's—with technological developments. Shipbuilders here, following and expanding the already highly advanced European shipbuilding tradition, while exploiting the enormous supplies of cheap and easily harvested timber, enjoyed a "Golden Age" of market dominance from the Colonial period until the Civil War. Long

Island provides both a microcosm of the national shipbuilding experience and a case study of how a peripheral region could adopt and benefit from the national pattern. But Long Island reveals something the national experience does not. It demonstrates how practitioners of an archaic industry could maximize opportunities on their waterfronts to perpetuate their craft after it had become extinct in its areas of former strength. The lower costs of Long Island shipbuilding made this possible.

The appearance in mid-century of government-subsidized, metal-hulled vessels in the United Kingdom altered the course of ship design and construction and doomed wooden shipbuilding. It put an end to wood as the material of choice for ocean-going ships, and it quickly finished American dominance in the trade. By 1870, shipbuilding had virtually vanished from its former strongholds in the great seaports along America's eastern seaboard. But Long Island shipbuilders enjoyed an "Indian Summer" in this technically outmoded business, and maintained their enterprises in generally prosperous conditions for another generation. Their methods of compensating for an increasingly disadvantageous competitive position are revealing—if not comforting. The Long Island shipbuilders exploited to the fullest one of the major advantages their peripheral position gave them over the fallen metropolitan giants. Low costs once again provided the essential ingredient for survival and affluence. After mid-century the lower costs were not in raw materials but in the wages the shipbuilders paid their laborers.

Nevertheless, neither the shipbuilders' successful suppression of wage increases nor their desultory attempts at government subsidy or protection for a doomed industry could forestall the fate of their trade indefinitely. The inability of Long Island shipbuilders to stave off the inexorable march of technological and economic change and innovation provides food for thought when pondering the futures of such troubled American industries as textiles, shoes, possibly even automobiles.

The transformative forces that closed Long Island's shipyards similarly altered its villages, its society and its very landscape. In the end, this exploration of Long Island wooden shipbuilding is a visit to a vanished world—one which resonates weakly in our own but has much to reveal about how our world evolved and where it might be going.

Acknowledgements

The creation of a book the size and scope of *An Island's Trade* would have been impossible without the generous assistance of many people. While gathering primary resource materials I was able to draw on the collections and expertise of the Huntington and Brookhaven Town Historian's Offices and the Three Village Public Library in Setauket. The staffs at the Huntington and Suffolk County Historical Societies and the Port Jefferson Public Library were most accommodating in providing guidance to their collections of local newspapers and documents. Thanks are also due to the Northport, Port Jefferson and Three Village Historical Societies for permitting the reproduction of many of the fine photographs from their archives. The Baker Library, Harvard Business School, was especially helpful in allowing me to quote from the records of R.G. Dun and Company. A special debt of gratitude is owed Frank and Frances Child who gave me complete access to their marvelous collection of Bayles family memorabilia. The Child Collection, as I refer to it in the book, represents the largest surviving documentary and photographic resource relating to any of the major nineteenth-century shipbuilding families of Long Island.

My researches into the history of last-century shipbuilding on Long Island would not have been undertaken without the help, guidance, and sometimes the cajolery of several members of the faculty of the History Department at the State University of New York at Stony Brook. My two major advisors, Ned Landsman and Eric Lampard, played essential mentoring and nurturing roles as I struggled to complete the dissertation on which this current work is based. In a similiar manner I would like to express my gratitude to Gerald E. Morris, formerly Director of Mystic Seaport's Publications Department, who first saw a book in my dissertation. This project could not have been brought to fruition without the talent, energy, goodwill and patience of Joseph Gribbins, current Director of Publications at Mystic Seaport, who oversaw the not-inconsiderable task of transforming an academic work into a publishable book.

Lastly, thanks to my understanding family who allowed me to retreat from domestic responsibilities to wrestle with my notes and word processor.

Richard F. Welch
Huntington, New York

CHAPTER ONE

Nineteenth-Century Shipbuilding on Long Island

The building of ships on Long Island is almost as old as European settlement. The great abundance of readily harvestable timber made this trade one of the more successful colonial enterprises. By 1730, fully a third of Britain's merchant fleet was constructed in the North American colonies.[1] Although it lagged behind New England, New York also shared in the colonial shipbuilding economy. While Manhattan was the center of New York's shipbuilding trades, Long Islanders engaged in them as well. The first record of a ship being built on Long Island appears in 1694. Six vessels—five sloops and a bark—were constructed between that year and 1707.[2] Although other vessels which escaped numeration may have been built in this formative period of the area's history, it seems certain their number could not have been large. Existing records show a total production of 1332 ships in the British North American colonies during the 1694-1707 period,[3] so even if the Long Island documentation is incomplete the Island's contribution would still be small. There is no indication of any embryonic shipbuilding center emerging on Long Island at this time—or indeed at any time during the eighteenth century. The only specific locations mentioned for this first thirteen-year span are Gardiner's Island, Southold and Cow Neck (Port Washington), none of which later developed into areas of ship construction. The greater part of the eighteenth century saw only sporadic shipbuilding on the Island, again without the establishment of any center for the industry or any continuing firm or family enterprise.

Although shipbuilding would not appear as an important undertaking on Long Island until the 1840s, the last decade of the eighteenth century witnessed some tentative steps in certain localities toward the establishment of a shipbuilding tradition. The first area to see wooden shipbuilding established as a major economic activity was the Setauket-Port Jefferson (Drowned Meadow) section of Brookhaven Town in western Suffolk County. Shipbuilding in this region was carried on least extensively in Stony Brook, more actively in Setauket, and became the most important trade in Port Jefferson for the bulk of the nineteenth century. Indeed, Port Jefferson emerged as the leading shipbuilding center on Long Island, Brooklyn excluded.

The first indication of a developing shipbuilding industry in these three villages occurred in 1787 when Benjamin Floyd constructed a large vessel named *Boyne* in Setauket. *Boyne* could carry seventy-two passengers and sailed an unscheduled New York-to-London-to-Amsterdam run.[4] Floyd does not seem to have continued his shipbuilding activity, although his example may have served to advertise the advantages of Setauket harbor to the next generation of men who established yards there in the 1820s. An anonymous merchant-shipbuilder was active in the Stony Brook area in the 1820s. While he established no permanently enduring yard he, like Floyd, may have called attention to the possibilities of the area for later practitioners. About the same time Floyd was constructing his *Boyne*, a more important development in Long Island shipbuilding was taking place a few miles to the east in what was then known as Drowned Meadow.

In 1779 John Willse arrived from Fort Lee, New Jersey, and took up residence at Jacob Van Brundt's farm at George's Neck, now Poquott. Only fourteen at the time, Willse may have come to the British-occupied Island because of a Tory background. In this backwater, he survived the American triumph four years later and by 1796 was building ships on the Van Brundt property.[5] In 1797, Willse bought land in the southeast corner of what is today Port Jefferson harbor from Judge Thomas Strong. In that same year he launched the first vessel from what was to become the Island's principal shipbuilding center. This was the provocatively named *King George*, perhaps an indication of ineradicable political convictions. She was a forty-ton sloop designed for the cordwood trade. Willse went on to launch at least five other vessels from this yard.[6]

In 1807, seeking better facilities for his maritime enterprises, which included shellfishing as well as shipbuilding, Willse petitioned the Town of Brookhaven for permission to build a dock. Permission was granted and the dock was built in 1809. Sometime before then, Richard Mather, and probably Mather's brother, Titus, apprenticed under Willse. Richard later married Willse's eldest daughter, Irena, and their son, John Richard, was born in 1814. By this time Richard Mather had constructed five sloops and had become the settlement's largest shipbuilder, eclipsing his father-in-law, when Willse died in 1815. Mather himself died shortly after in an accident during the construction of the sloop *Catherine Rogers*. Yet this family-dominated shipbuilding business at Drowned Meadow continued. William L. Jones, who had apprenticed with Titus Mather, married Richard's widow, Willse's daughter. Jones built two vessels during the 1820s. And his stepson John R. Mather helped initiate the shipbuilding boom in Port Jefferson during the 1840s when he was joined by the Darlings, Bayleses and other, more peripheral, builders. Indeed as the accompanying chart (The Willse Connection, page 3) shows, the interrelationships caused by family and apprenticeship patterns is striking.

Port Jefferson's closest competitor, Northport, had a slightly later start. There is no record of shipbuilding there until about 1812 when a builder known as C. Beebee engaged in the trade. About 1820 Isaac Scudder Ketcham constructed ships in Northport Harbor, and in 1828 a firm named Bunce and

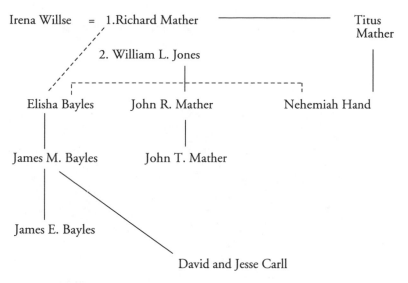

Irena Willse = 1.Richard Mather ———————— Titus
                                                Mather
              2. William L. Jones

Elisha Bayles   John R. Mather   Nehemiah Hand

James M. Bayles   John T. Mather

James E. Bayles

                   David and Jesse Carll

Straight lines denote known relationships. Broken lines indicate presumed linkages.

The Willse Connection

Bayles was active.[7] Whether the Bayles of Bunce and Bayles was related to the important Bayles family of Port Jefferson or to David Bayles, a Setauket builder, is not known. Despite the appearance of these firms, another decade would pass before Northport's major shipbuilders, Jesse Jarvis, the Hartts and the Carlls, would set up their yards. Records relating to Suffolk's remaining shipbuilding village, Greenport, are most elusive, and there is no indication of shipbuilding there before the middle of the nineteenth century.

Shipbuilding on Long Island, excluding Brooklyn, which was geographically and economically part of the port of New York, was essentially a North Shore activity. Two of the three major shipbuilding towns, Northport and Setauket-Port Jefferson, lie on Long Island Sound while the third, Greenport, is situated on the Peconic Bay side of the North Fork. Hence the North Shore quality of the enterprise remains consistent. Topography, not any special advantage in talent possessed by North Shore residents, dictated the North Shore orientation of the business. The Sound shoreline of Long Island is blessed with several deep fjord-like harbors gouged out by the retreating glaciers. These bays provided protective settings which attracted the earliest settlements and villages whose residents supported themselves in part by fishing. During the nineteenth century such settings proved a natural and desirable location for the production of ships. The sheltered bays provided places where ships could be constructed without damage or interruption, and yet be floated out directly onto one of the nation's major marine thoroughfares. The more placid nature of Long Island Sound, as compared to the Atlantic, added to the attractions of the North Shore by providing generally calmer conditions for sea trials. The South Shore of

Long Island, lined by great barrier beaches from Brooklyn to Shinnecock, lacked the deep protected harbors so convenient for shipbuilding. The Great South Bay and Moriches Bay, which lie between the South Shore and the barrier beaches, are generally too shallow for large, heavy vessels. The South Shore also had fewer villages, a smaller population and less commercial activity.

The full-rigged ship Adorna, *built for the cotton trade by David B. Bayles in 1870. (Another* Adorna *was begun in 1876 and not finished as a sailing ship.)*

Patchogue, on the South Shore of Brookhaven Town, did become an active boatbuilding area during the second half of the nineteenth century. However, its production was much more specialized and localized, primarily serving the needs of the Great South Bay fishing and shellfishing industry.

Several other Suffolk villages engaged spasmodically in shipbuilding, and very rarely a vessel was launched from a Queens County village. But none of these places approached the three major centers in either quantity or persistence. Some villages that would appear to have had as great a potential as Northport, Setauket or Port Jefferson remained minor shipbuilding areas or never developed the trade at all. With their whaling ships and protected harbors, Sag Harbor and Cold Spring Harbor, as ports of entry, would seem likely candidates for the shipbuilding industry. Sag Harbor, although one of the nation's major whaling ports in the antebellum period, produced a mere handful of vessels. One of the firms known to have produced ships there, E.E. Smith, actually originated in Smithtown and moved to Sag Harbor in 1861.[8] Cold Spring Harbor, with its extremely deep, well-protected bay, offered the same possibilities as Northport and Port Jefferson. Although some shipbuilding was carried on there between 1830 and 1870, the total output lagged far behind

SCHR. ROYAL ARCH J. D. HAWKINS MASTER LEAVING THE PORT of PALERMO

The three-masted schooner Royal Arch, *built by another David Bayles — David T. — in 1867. This portrait of her was painted in Palermo, Sicily, in 1869.*

Northport, and no Cold Spring builder ever rose to prominence as did the ship-builders farther east.

Although shipbuilding in Suffolk County showed potential by the 1820s, the effects of the war of 1812, the financial panic of 1819, and continued exclusion from the British mercantilist system which denied commerce with British ports and outposts to non-British vessels, retarded the development of the industry. Not surprisingly, the extent of the Island's shipbuilding activity remained far behind the immediate center of the trade in New York City. In 1825, Manhattan had twenty shipyards, with 6000 men employed, and the great days still lay ahead.[9] By contrast, in that same year only Port Jefferson showed any consistent activity, and that was confined to two or three builders who produced one ship a year during the first five years of the 1820s.[10]

If the 1820s saw the foundation of wooden shipbuilding on Long Island,

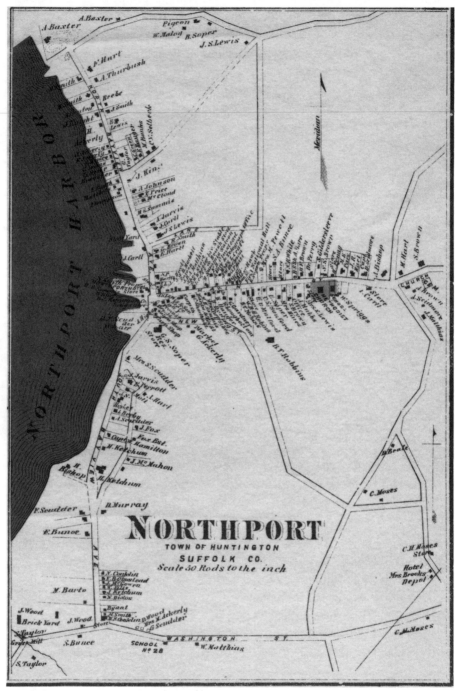

Northport in 1873.

PORT JEFFERSON

TOWN OF BROOKHAVEN
SUFFOLK CO.
Scale 18 Rods to the inch

Port Jefferson in 1873.

the real growth began in the 1840s. The "Golden Age" of wooden shipbuilding in America was the decade between 1847 and 1857. Between 1830 and 1861, tonnage produced in American shipyards increased fivefold from 1,191,776 to 5,539,813. The latter figure would not be surpassed in the United States until 1902.[11] This prodigious expansion was accomplished by a multiplication of the number of shipyards rather than economy of scale. By the mid-1850s, hundreds of shipyards dotted the Atlantic seaboard, primarily north of the Delaware River.[12] After 1857, depression and then the Civil War had an adverse effect on demand. The industry revived after the war, but became even more specialized geographically, with many former areas of production falling by the wayside. By the 1880s the long-delayed triumph of steam, along with the increasing use of metal hulls, forced out companies and villages that could not adopt the new technologies. Lastly, subsidized foreign fleets captured much of the market formerly held by American shipping, and the American merchant fleet dwindled precipitously. Only the spectacular conditions of the First and Second World Wars caused a renewed expansion of the American merchant fleet, and such growth lasted only as long as the emergency that provoked it.

Long Island benefitted from the burgeoning shipbuilding industry of the antebellum period. In addition to the advantage of its indented North Shore coastline, Long Island originally possessed some of the woods desirable in ship construction. After 1812, American shipwrights generally used white oak for nearly every component of a ship—frames, keel, outside planking, waterways, rails and, to a lesser extent, ceilings and beams. Pitch pine—yellow pine—came into use in the 1830s for beams, and was later used for ceilings and keels. Yellow pine was used extensively for planking and other components of later ships.[13] When shipbuilding first became an important endeavor on Long Island, native oak was available for the framing, and the bosses sometimes selected likely trees during slack winter periods.[14] Local cedar was occasionally used for the knees that served as braces between the ribs and the deck beams. Long Island locust sometimes saw use in framing and, right up to the demise of the industry, for trunnels (treenails or dowels used as fastenings).

After the 1830s the supply of usable timber in New England and Long Island began to dwindle and southern lumber gradually became the mainstay of the shipbuilders. Pitch pine from the Chesapeake region became the major ingredient in wooden shipbuilding. Pitch pine was the favored wood for all parts of vessels over 100 tons except the keel, frames, stem and stempost. Oak or other hardwood was still preferred for frame members, while white pine or spruce was selected for masts.[15] Long Island seems to have weathered the shift from local to southern woods during the 1830-1860 period. Certainly by the 1880s prime shipbuilding lumber was very scarce on the Island and second- or third-growth oak and locust were too small for anything but stanchions and trunnels. Occasionally, however, local wood might be used for specific vessels.

In 1874 a white oak described as twelve feet in diameter—almost certainly twelve feet in circumference, not diameter—was cut in Middleville, south of Northport, for a yacht. The tree, which was sold to a "Mr. Hart"—probably Samuel Prior Hartt or his son, Erastus—fetched fifty dollars.[16] By the late nineteenth century the selection of prime timber on Long Island for ship construction was unusual enough to be recorded.

A good indication of the relative importance of the various woods and their value was given in the 1870 Census of Manufactures. The census taker recorded a breakdown of the materials used by six Setauket-Port Jefferson shipbuilders:

chestnut	232,000 feet	$6,300
yellow pine	180,000	10,300
white pine	119,000	7,400
white oak	108,000	61,350
locust	20,800	4,300

Source: United States Census of Manufacturers, Port Jefferson, 1870

Significantly, the most expensive wood was the increasingly scarce, but still indispensable, white oak. The most commonly used wood, chestnut, was also the cheapest. For as long as it was available, chestnut was frequently used in place of oak for the keels, stems, deadwood and other main frame members of vessels. Unfortunately, the American chestnut was destined to be virtually extinct within 30 years due to the chestnut blight. The second most commonly used wood, yellow pine, another name for pitch pine, and a wood widely used not only in ship construction but for wharves and the beams of buildings, was a southern tree and would have been brought north in bulk.

Several factors combined to create the great antebellum shipping boom in which Long Island shipbuilders shared. In 1849, reacting to the potato famine in Ireland, Great Britain repealed the Navigation Acts, thus opening the imperial system to American-owned and American-built vessels. This measure gave rise to a flourishing grain trade between Britain and the United States, which was carried out primarily in American-built ships. British shippers also took the opportunity to purchase cheaper American-built vessels.[17] Heavy immigration from Ireland and Germany also increased a demand for ships which American builders were happy to satisfy. Domestically, the rapid rise of cotton as the United States' leading export fueled the shipbuilding boom. Exports of raw cotton doubled between 1830 and 1840, then tripled between 1840 and 1860.[18] More vessels were needed to ship the fiber to Europe, and with New York City's dominant position in the cotton trade it is likely that some of the shipyards on Long Island contributed to this commerce. Lastly, the discovery of gold near Sacramento created an almost instantaneous demand for transportation to California, which expanded the market for sailing vessels even further.

American shipbuilders also benefitted from lower construction costs, partly a result of the plentiful supply of cheap lumber. In 1825, a 300-ton vessel cost

The three-masted schooner Fleetwing, *built in 1855. She was converted to a barkentine in 1860.*

$75-80 per ton in the United States, $90-100 per ton in Canada and $100-110 in England.[19] In 1847, the cost of a large and first-class ship had not changed in the United States, and although British costs had fallen to $87-90 per ton, the United States retained it competitive advantage.[20]

Long Island-built ships took part in many of the major areas of sea commerce characteristic of nineteenth-century economic life—delivering settlers and gold-seekers to California, shipping America's cotton to England, trading with Latin America, and interoceanic whaling. But from its beginnings in the 1820s a staple of Long Island shipbuilding was the American coastal trade, closed to foreign ships since 1818. The coastal trade was ordinarily undertaken in small- to medium-sized vessels, which carried freight between cities and towns along the Atlantic and Gulf coast. During much of the nineteenth century overland shipping was literally primitive, with few good roads and only small wagonloads of cargo before the advent of railroads. And even the railroads could not compete with much of the port-to-port coasting traffic during most of the nineteenth century. The vessel most commonly used for coasting was the efficient and remarkably adaptable schooner. Schooners became, in fact, the most common vessel turned out by Long Island shipyards. Schooners had not always dominated the coasting trade. Before 1840 sloops were the most frequently used coasting vessels. They were simple in every way, built up and down the Atlantic coast, and could be managed by three men. However, sloop design was not adaptable to medium or large-sized ships—vessels to carry more cargo—and so ketches, brigantines and three-masted schooners were used in longer runs and for cargos such as lumber where greater capacity was important. Between 1840 and 1850 large, square-rigged coasters such as brigs and barks saw limited use. By 1860, maritime design had become specialized. The steamers increasingly took the passenger and mail service, and the schooners of two and three masts dominated the coastal trade.[21]

Schooner design evolved to meet the changing demands placed upon it. The general tendency was toward larger vessels as the trade grew and larger cargos were carried. The earlier schooners from the antebellum period tended to be no more than 50 tons. After 1860, two-masters ranged from 100 to 250 tons and three-masters from 300 to 750 tons. The predominant Atlantic-coast schooner of the c. 1860-1890 period was a three-masted and generally flat-bottomed vessel of about 600 tons.[22] One of the main attractions of schooner design was its adaptability. Schooners with four, five, or even seven masts were built as the schooner era progressed into the new century. In 1880 it was estimated that more schooners were constructed in the United States than all other types combined.[23] Another of the schooner's virtues—and perhaps the principal one in its roughly 60-year history as an important cargo-carrier—was its ability to be managed by a small crew. The schooner's many small and manageable sails could be struck or set by a few men, in contrast to the large crews required by square-rigged vessels such as barks and brigs. The small schooner managed by "two men and a boy" was part of coastal folklore. And although they clearly dominated the coastal trade, many American schooners made ocean passages.

Between the burgeoning coastal trade, the expanding transoceanic commerce, and the enormous demands of California traffic, the years between 1840 and 1855 were a halcyon period for American shipbuilders. The building boom extended from the great centers of New York and Boston to the lesser ports of the U.S. coast from Maine to Mississippi. Seen in its proper scale, the expansion of Long Island shipbuilding was just as impressive. In 1840, when it was estimated that Suffolk County's investment in the industry was $70,000,[24] there were not many more than 20 builders in the County. Two of these were partnerships, and several were clearly only occasional builders constructing as few as two vessels in a 20-year period.[25] But by 1855, which may have been the peak year for shipbuilding locally and nationally, the situation had greatly changed (Table 1-1, page 13). Suffolk County then counted 25 shipbuilding establishments. While only a small numerical increase over the 20-odd builders of 1840, the scale of these operations had grown. Brookhaven Town, with three important centers at Setauket, Port Jefferson and Patchogue, ranked highest with 14 firms. Southold Town was next with five, and Huntington Town was right behind with four. Islip and Smithtown had only one shipbuilding establishment each.[26] Brookhaven Town's yards reported a real-estate value of $16,700, and the value of their tools was estimated at $2655. The stock of construction materials for shipbuilding in Brookhaven was valued at $118,045, and its products were estimated to be worth $281,500. Some 236 men earned their living in Brookhaven shipyards.[27] This was a shipbuilding industry indeed in a town like Brookhaven whose 1850 population numbered 8595 and whose other industries were service trades for the agricultural population.

Although Southold had one more shipyard than Huntington, the scale of the latter's establishments was considerably greater. Huntington Town outstripped Southold Town in the real-estate value of its yards $16,000 to $6500, and its tool value $1800 to $1650. The value of Huntington's raw materials at hand exceeded that of Southold $51,500 to $1700. Huntington's vessels were worth $191,000 as opposed to Southold's $18,300.[28] Huntington employed 125 men in its shipyards; Southold provided jobs for 40. Islip Town's shipbuilders employed 18 men and produced $17,000 worth of vessels in 1855. The one shipbuilder in Smithtown supplied no information other than a $500 estimate for the value of his tools.[29]

It is clear that by 1855 shipbuilding had made great strides in Suffolk County, which had constructed a minimum of 15 percent of the total number of vessels built in New York State in 1855.[30] This growth was not confined to Suffolk County. Kings County—the Brooklyn waterfront—had only six firms, yet the scale of its activities went well beyond anything in the rest of Long Island. The real estate value of the Kings County yards in 1855 was $411,000, compared to which Brookhaven's $16,700 and Huntington's $16,000 were fractions, and Brooklyn had $42,000 invested in tools. Raw materials stored in Kings County shipyards were valued at $579,000 in 1855, and the vessels they produced that year were worth $945,000. Five hundred forty men labored in the Brooklyn shipyards versus 419 in all of Suffolk.[31] Queens County had only one yard in Newtown Town with an assessed census real estate value of $45,000, machines and tools worth $60,000, $26,580 invested in raw materials, and vessels worth $130,000. Twenty-five men worked there.[32] No doubt the very high real-estate values of the shipyards in Kings and Queens reflected the generally higher real-estate values close to the metropolis.

By way of contrast, New York City had only as many shipyards as Suffolk—25. However, the scale of its enterprises was even greater than that of Kings County across the East River. The real estate value of New York's shipyards was $673,000, with $57,300 invested in tools and facilities. The City's shipbuilders owned $922,816 in raw materials and produced vessels valued at $2,593,761 in 1855.[33] In comparison, the combined total of all Long-Island-built ships was $1,582,761 that year. The City outproduced Long Island by more than $1,000,000. Manhattan yards employed 1733 men, almost double the Long

	Number of Establishments	Capital Real Estate	Invested Tools	Raw Materials	Vessels	Employees
New York City	25	$673,000	$57,300	$922,816	$2,593,761	1,733
Kings	6	411,000	42,000	579,000	945,000	540
Queens (Newtown)	1	45,000	60,000	26,580	130,000	25
Suffolk (Brookhaven)	14	16,700	2,655	118,045	281,500	236
Huntington	4	16,100	1,800	51,500	191,000	125
Smithtown	1		500			
Islip	1		2,000	11,702	17,000	18
Southold	5	6,500	4,650	17,000	18,300	40
Suffolk Total	25					419
Long Island Total	32					984

Source: New York State Census, 1855.

TABLE 1-1
Shipbuilding on Long Island and in New York City, 1855

Island total of 984[34] As important as they were to their local economies, the Long Island shipyards, especially those in Suffolk County, were second-level concerns compared to such Manhattan giants as William Webb and Smith and Dimon. However, when the disparities in population between Suffolk County and New York City are taken into account, the volume and monetary value of Suffolk's builders compare favorably to that of the City. The importance of shipbuilding to the economies of specific Suffolk towns and villages must have been greater than that of Manhattan shipbuilding to the diverse economy of New York City.

The backbone of the shipbuilding industry on Long Island and elsewhere was the force of shipwrights, shipsmiths, caulkers, painters, riggers and other specialists who built and rigged the ships. The size of the different workforces, as listed in Table 1-2, testifies again to the enormous scale of the industry in New York and the contiguous Brooklyn waterfront. The total of Long Island's ship carpenters barely exceeded the New York contingent 1244 to 1146. The figures also demonstrate that Suffolk County comprised a discrete shipbuilding area. Only one yard in western Queens lay between the Brooklyn shipyards and the most westerly Suffolk yard at Cold Spring Harbor. Surprisingly, the census figures report no shipsmiths in Suffolk. While Suffolk's builders are known to have patronized ship's chandlers and smiths in the center of things along the Brooklyn and Manhattan waterfronts, it seems unlikely that such an essential trade remained nonexistent in Suffolk. They may have operated as integral parts of the shipyards and were not counted as separate establishments. At least four are mentioned in the business directories from the 1864-74 period in Port Jefferson.[35] Another industry ancillary to shipbuilding was spar manufacturing. Suffolk had three such businesses in 1855, two in Southold and one in East Hampton. Their five-man labor force produced $3800 worth of goods that

	Ship carpenters	Sailmakers	Shipsmiths	Shipriggers	Total
New York	1,146	281	168	86	1,681
Kings	875	177	7		1,059
Queens	40	2			42
Suffolk	329	19			348
Total	2,390	479	175	86	3,310
Long Island Total	1,244	198	7		1,449

Source: New York State Census, 1855

TABLE 1-2

Numbers Employed in the Major Shipbuilding Trades, 1855

year. New York City had only three spar manufacturers, but even here its economy of scale was overwhelming. The 95 men engaged in this trade turned out spars valued at $310,000 in 1855.[36] Certain specialized shipworkers such as caulkers were not enumerated.

Although steam-driven vessels had existed since the early part of the nineteenth century, in mid-century they still had not captured the bulk-cargo trade from sail, which retained its advantage in that area until the end of the century. Steam was used heavily in passenger traffic on the Hudson River and Long Island Sound, and was beginning to see increasing use in trans-Atlantic passenger runs in the late antebellum period. Only one shipyard, in Brooklyn, was devoted to steamboat construction in mid-century. This yard, employing 64 men, produced vessels worth $150,000 in 1855.[37]

The year 1855 may have seen the merchant fleet and the shipbuilding industry of the United States at their heights. The decade between 1855 and 1865 certainly witnessed a precipitate decline in both. Several factors combined to cause this contraction. The decline is partly attributable to overproduction during the 1845-55 period.[38] Many ships had been ordered for the California run after the discovery of gold in 1848. However, by 1855 the gold mania had cooled, and both passenger and freight service to California fell off as well. Steam had begun to take much of the passenger service away from sail by mid-century, and added mail and express freight to its list of conquests.

Nature also dealt shipping a heavy blow in the winter of 1856-1857 when disastrous storms destroyed 400 vessels worth more than a million dollars.[39] While the loss of so many vessels might have been expected to trigger a renewed demand for ships, high world prices served to depress trade and keep exports in check. The Civil War also acted as a retardant to trade and consequently to shipbuilding. An exception to wartime depression in the New York region was Brooklyn, since several of its shipyards specialized in the construction of ironclads and monitors for the United States Navy. All in all, the eight-year period between 1857 and 1865 was unfavorable for the production of ships of large tonnage. In fact, these years almost brought a premature end to the American shipbuilding industry and heralded the decline of United States shipping activities generally.[40]

The contraction of shipbuilding can be measured by comparing the statistics from the 1855 state census with those from 1865 (Table 1-3, page 16). Unfortunately, the categories reported and the information presented in the 1865 census are not as detailed as those from 1855. Nevertheless, the pattern of decline shows clearly enough. In addition to the categories listed in Table 1-3 there were also trunnel (treenail) manufacturers, one in Kings and one in Queens, with a total output of $31,500.[41]

The most striking decline took place in Manhattan, where shipbuilding was soon to be extinct. Queens lost its yard in Newtown and, if the figures are accurate, only Brookhaven and Huntington Towns retained any shipyards in Suffolk. Brookhaven suffered a serious reduction in the number of firms—from 14 to four. Some of that reduction may simply reflect consolidation and concentration of the industry in the hands of the more capable builders. In contrast, Huntington Town remained relatively stable in the number of reported shipyards, with a loss of only one from its 1855 figure. Yet the cash value of its ships crashed from $191,000 to $18,000. The decline was even worse in terms of value, since the Civil War years brought a significant inflation. Price levels rose 64 percent between 1855 and 1865, rendering Huntington's $18,000 for 1865 a very weak figure.[42]

The one bright spot in the general pattern of contraction lay in Kings. Both the number of shipyards and the value of vessels constructed increased spectacularly along the Brooklyn waterfront. This was to prove a temporary aberration produced by the Civil War. The demand for warships by the Navy, particularly steam vessels and ironclads, was responsible for Brooklyn's stupendous, but brief, shipbuilding boom. Aside from the Brooklyn Navy Yard itself, which was a federal installation, there were at least four other Kings County yards constructing vessels on government order. A report from the autumn of 1863 lists a monitor and a steam sloop under construction in two different yards and goes on to say "...a large number of ocean and Sound steamers (both side wheel and propeller), ferry boats and wooden vessels were being constructed in the various yards."[43] In its March 17, 1864, edition, the Brooklyn *Union* reported that "the estimated value of vessels now building at Greenpoint, including those from the government, is upwards of ten million dollars, and the number of persons employed thereon is between two and three thousand."[44] The prosperity the Civil War brought to Brooklyn dissipated soon after Appomattox. By 1880 the few remaining shipyards in Kings were building only small boats or doing repair work. Unfortunately, the New York Census for 1865 does not provide a breakdown for the number of men employed in the various shipyards. Some attempt can be made to gauge the size of the workforce by consulting the United States Population Censuses. Even so, comparison of these figures with New York State returns is not entirely satisfactory since they were taken five years apart and give

	SHIPBUILDERS		SPAR MAKERS	
	Number	Value of Products	Number	Value of Products
Kings	10	$2,120,800	1	$50,000
Queens				
Suffolk (Brookhaven)	4	196,000		
Suffolk (Huntington)	3	18,000		
Total	17	2,334,800	1	50,000
New York	5	805,000	2	45,000

Source: New York State Census, 1865

TABLE 1-3

Shipbuilding on Long Island and in New York City, 1865

different numbers. For example, the Suffolk County returns show relative stability between 1860 and 1870, with a pronounced decline between 1870 and 1880 (see Table 1-4). Certainly the prewar decade appears to have been the most expansive after mid-century.

Several conclusions may be drawn from the statistics in Table 1-4. The first is that Suffolk weathered the 1855-65 period without the severe depression experienced to the west. State returns do show a decline in both number of establishments and total output between 1855 and 1865; but federal population statistics, reporting only a slight decrease in the workforce from 1860 to 1870, probably reflect the persistence of wooden shipbuilding activity in some areas after the war ended. One of those areas was Long Island. The United States population census indicates that Suffolk's shipbuilding strength was based in Southold, and especially in Brookhaven Town. In contrast, Huntington Town's shipyard occupations declined by a third. The general stability of the Suffolk shipbuilding workers probably owed something to the independence of Suffolk yards from war-related work and the concomitant boom and bust that destroyed shipbuilding in New York Harbor. There seems little doubt that Suffolk shipbuilding benefitted from lower labor costs, and this small economic advantage had probably furthered the viability of peripheral shipbuilding centers since the colonial period.[45] It served the Suffolk yards well in the 1860s. The County's yards turned out a minimum of 23 percent of the state's total ship production in 1865.[46]

Kings County shipbuilding, which had boomed in the 1860s, is poorly chronicled and, apparently, poorly remembered. The histories of Long Island compiled at the end of the century scarcely mention it. Stiles' *History of the County of Kings and City of Brooklyn* (1884) does not mention shipbuilding at all.[47] Certainly the industry faded rapidly after 1865. In 1880, Brooklyn was still credited with ten yards, but all were devoted to the construction of vessels such as tugboats, lighters, pilot boats and yachts.[48]

The sharp decline of shipbuilding in Kings County was exceeded by the total

	1850	1860	1870	1880
Huntington	2	66	47	49
Brookhaven	48	151	127	92
Southold	30	23	44	35
All Others	29	28	33	24
Total Suffolk	109	268	251	200

Source: U.S. Population Censuses 1850,1860,1870,1880.

TABLE 1-4
Numbers Reported as Working in Suffolk County Shipyards

collapse of the trade in New York City, which had been one of the great national centers of the industry. The construction of sailing vessels practically ceased in all the major shipbuilding cities during the Civil War. According to census reporter Henry Hall, high labor costs and labor turmoil after the war prevented the industry from reviving.[49] By 1880 shipbuilding in Manhattan was described as "extinct,"[50] although it survived longer in Brooklyn.

Outside the large cities the picture was not so gloomy. Even as steam and metal hulls continued their inexorable rise to dominance, sailing vessels continued to carry most of the protected long-haul cargos and the bulk-cargo coasting trade into the new century. Only at the end of the nineteenth century did the triple-expansion engine decisively tilt the advantage to steam and seal the fate of wooden sailing vessels.[51] Due to continued modifications and improvements, competitive construction costs achieved through falling wages, and competitive carrying charges in long-haul routes, wooden sailing vessels remained viable for another 40 years after the Civil War. Consequently, between 1865 and 1880 there was a renewal of the American shipbuilding industry. If not on the same scale as the 1840-55 boom, this "Indian Summer" was significant enough in the long history of trade under sail in North America and the short history of its decline between 1860 and 1920.

The post-1865 revival was generally a result of the eight-year retraction in construction which had reduced the national inventory of sailing vessels. New ships were needed to meet the expansion of United States foreign trade after 1865, with domestic coasting and trade with other protected areas—Alaska, Hawaii, Puerto Rico and Cuba—remaining the industry's staple. The shipyards of Suffolk county were well-suited to take advantage of these postwar opportunities. Their location along the major traffic artery of Long Island Sound and close to one of the world's major trading centers was a significant advantage, and so were lower labor costs and the absence of real-estate pressures, both of which doomed the metropolitan yards. With Manhattan and Brooklyn priced out of the market, regional demand for sailing ships went to peripheral areas where both labor and materials were lower.[52]

The general consistency of the number of workers in the Suffolk yards between 1860 and 1870 testifies to the general health of the industry in the

County during that decade of shipbuilding revival. These figures also indicate that the industry did not begin to decline again before the late 1870s. But by 1880 shipbuilding in Suffolk County was clearly in trouble, and by 1890 only the biggest builders were able to continue at all.[53]

There are several indications of the downward movement of Long Island shipbuilding. One is found in the decline of the shipbuilding workforce as reported in the 1880 census—251 men listed shipbuilding trades for their occupations in 1870. Only 200 did so in 1880.[54] The number of builders listed in the various compilations also fell sharply from their 1850-1870 highs. The decline becomes even more pronounced after 1880. By that year Port Jefferson had only two full-time producers of vessels, John Titus Mather and James E. Bayles. Northport might claim three since it is unclear when Edward Lefferts quit the business. However, the scale of activity in the yards of Northport was much smaller than that of Port Jefferson and was primarily devoted to repair work. One of the Northport builders, Erastus Hartt, did not even build ships in the old Hartt yard, which had been sold. Instead he rented space in Jesse Carll's yard. Jesse Carll, Sr., who had been Northport's leading shipbuilder, had retired by the 1880s and his son, Jesse, Jr., ran the family concern. A few oyster steamers were built there, but the bulk of the business was in repairs. Shipbuilding did not live much past 1880 in Greenport. Nevertheless, some Long Island builders did try to adapt to the new steam technology, although their work was with lesser vessels than the coasting and deepwater ships that had built their shipyards. In Port Jefferson 40 of 43 vessels built between 1891 and 1917 were steam launches, recreational yachts, and such prosaic vessels as scows and lighters.[55] The days of producing real ships on Long Island had passed.

The *Report on Shipbuilding* compiled for the 1880 census by Henry Hall likewise paints a picture of a dying industry. According to Hall's *Report*, Greenport produced one barkentine and employed only a dozen shipwrights in 1880.[56] Henry Hall noted that in Port Jefferson, capital of Long Island shipbuilding, production had fallen from about 17 ships per yard in 1857 to six or seven in 1866, then declined to a total of four coasting schooners in 1880.[57] Similarly, the village's main sailmaker, Frederick Wilson, had employed 16 men and cut 50,000 yards of canvas a year before the Civil War; in 1880 he had only three men busy cutting 14,000 yards annually.[58] Port Jefferson's proximity to the City was judged useful in bringing in some work from that direction, but most of its construction was described as being steam and sail yachts. Steady repair work was credited with keeping the shipyards going and allowing the builders "to take an occasional contract at low figures."[59] No ships were reported built at either Setauket or Northport in 1880. An unfinished schooner-yacht was described as standing, unfinished, in its frames at Northport.[60]

Unfortunately, the New York State Industrial Census for 1875, which might have shed some light on the direction of shipbuilding, was aborted. The compi-

lations were judged "so incomplete and inexact as to be worthless for statistical purposes."[61] State officials contested and disbelieved the accuracy of the census figures since they showed that overall state manufactures had declined 27 percent from the 1865 mark[62] during a time of considerable economic expansion. A general state total of ship and boat builders was furnished, and this showed a drop from 229 in 1865 to 165 in 1875—a 69 percent decrease.[63] From what is known of the fate of shipbuilding in New York Harbor during this period, these statistics, at least, were probably accurate.

With the notable exception of Port Jefferson, complete lists of ships built on Long Island do not go past 1882. Nevertheless, the direction of the industry is clear. In 1871-75, Northport launched 13 vessels; in 1881-85 there were five launchings. During the same periods Port Jefferson's output fell from 38 to 16, and Greenport's dropped from five to one.[64] The number of shipbuilders fell as well. In 1870 there were seven builders in Northport, eleven in Port Jefferson and five in Greenport. In 1891 there were two builders in Port Jefferson, three in Northport and none in Greenport or Setauket. The Northport figure is deceptive since Edward Lefferts was a marginal builder and Erastus Hartt, as previously noted, had so little work he rented space in the Carll yard when he got a contract. By 1891 only James E. Bayles and John Titus Mather kept the industry alive in Port Jefferson.

The accelerating collapse of Long Island's shipbuilding industry was a local variation on a national theme. In the 1890s, the American merchant marine shrank dramatically as foreign-owned and -built ships took over more and more of the carrying trade. Meanwhile, coasting felt itself under pressure from railroads, and would soon be facing competition from vessels powered by the new

	Number of New Vessels	Tonnage	Value	Number of Boats	Value of Boats	Value of Repairs	Total Value
New York City	2	18	21,000	642	163,360	1,905,545	2,071,605
Kings	78	11,259	649,995	92	19,241	1,350,552	19,997,688
Queens	1	8	1,200				1,200
Suffolk	18	2,567	147,750	124	31,040	1,311,188	309,978
Total Long Island	97	13,834	798,945	216	50,281	1,481,740	2,310,966

Source: Henry Hall, *Report on Shipbuilding*, 1880

TABLE 1-5

Ship Production in New York City and Long Island, 1880

internal-combustion engine. As early as 1880, of the 7,000,000 tons of shipping which entered New York Harbor annually, only 1,500,000 represented American-built vessels.[65] The only bright spot in the increasingly bleak outlook for American shipping was Maine. Cheap timber, low wages, and proximity to the major fisheries led to Maine's continuance as the nation's premier shipbuilding state during the 1880s and 1890s. After it exhausted most of its easily exploitable timber, Maine retained first place among the nation's shipbuilding states through low wages and the "enterprise of her builders." In fact, Bath, Maine, was described by Henry Hall as "the principal shipbuilding town of the United States" in his 1884 report.[66] And even for Maine the writing was on the wall at the end of the 1890s.

On Long Island by the close of the century only the Carll yard hung on in Northport, surviving on repair work. During World War I, Jesse Carll, Jr. leased the premises to a company that built scows for the Navy. During the 1920s building ceased entirely and the shipyard was given to the village for use as a park. In the 1880s, the only regular shipbuilder in Greenport crossed Gardiner's Bay and became involved in the menhaden oil business in Promised Land. John Titus Mather kept building smaller and less-prestigious vessels—with the 1108-ton four-masted schooner *Martha E. Wallace* as a notable exception—until 1908. James E. Bayles constructed small power and pleasure craft until 1917 when he, too, sold out. Long Island's shipbuilding era had ended.

Notes:

1. Joseph A. Goldenberg, *Shipbuilding in Colonial America,* (Charlottesville, Va.: University of Virginia Press, 1976), 53.

2. United States Department of Commerce, Bureau of the Census, *United States Census of Population, 1880. Vol. VIII. The Shipbuilding Industry of the United States,* by Henry Hall. (Washington, DC, 1884), 59.

3. Ibid.

4. William Minuse, "Shipbuilding in Brookhaven Town." Taped lecture, March 21, 1975. Suffolk County Historical Society.

5. Welles and Prios, *Port Jefferson, Story of a Village* (Port Jefferson: Historical Society of Greater Port Jefferson, 1927)

6. Ibid.

7. Ramonah Sammis, *Huntington-Babylon Town History* (Huntington: Huntington Historical Society, 1937), 165.

8. Henry D. Sleight (ed.), *Town Records of the Town of Smithtown* Vol. I (Smithtown, 1929), 297.

9. Welles and Prios, 8.

10. Ibid.

11. Hutchins, John G.B., *The American Maritime Industries and Public Policy, 1789-1914* (Cambridge Mass: Harvard University Press, 1941), 71.

12. Ibid., 31.

13. Hall, 64.

14. William Minuse, *Shipbuilding in Setauket* Privately printed, 1955, 6, and Hall, 119.

15. Hall, 87.

16. Sleight, 297.

17. Robert G. Albion, "Foreign Trade in the Era of Wooden Ships" in Harold F. Williamson

(ed.) *The Growth of the American Economy* (Englewood Cliffs: Prentice-Hall, 1957), 222.

18. Ibid., 219.

19. Hall, 87.

20. Ibid.

21. Ibid., 93.

22. Ibid., 94.

23. Ibid.

24. Ralph Gabriel, *The Evolution of Long Island*, 1921, 129.

25. *Bi-Centennial History of Suffolk County* (Babylon: Budget Steam Print, 1885), 106-125. A totally accurate listing of all Long Island-built ships has yet to be printed. The number constructed after 1855 has been approximated with some degree of accuracy, but statistics before that date are problematical. The basic source for Long Island-built ships is the shipbuilding appendix to the *Bi-Centennial History* of 1885, which is relied upon by most authorities.

26. *Census of the State of New York for 1855.* (Albany: Charles Van Benthuysen, 1857), 378.

27. Ibid.

28. Ibid.

29. Ibid.

30. Ibid., 436, BCH, 115-122 and Welles and Prios, 76-81. See also Appendix I.

31. Ibid.

32. Ibid.

33. Ibid.

34. Ibid.

35. *Boyd's Directory of Long Island, New York*, 1864-65, 7.

36. *New York State Census*, 1855, 358.

37. Ibid.

38. Hall, 92.

39. Ibid.

40. Ibid.

41. *Census of the State of New York for 1865* (Albany: Charles Van Benthuysen & Sons, 1867), 439.

42. Consumer Price Index, 1800-1900, United States Department of Commerce, Bureau of Census, *Historical Statistics of the United States, Colonial Times to 1970,* Vol. I (Washington, D.C., 1975), 210-211.

43. Ross, *History of Long Island*, Vol. I, 439.

44. Ibid.

45. Goldenberg, 95.

46. New York State Census for 1865, 39, BCH, 115-122, Welles and Prios, 76-81. Also see Appendix I.

47. Henry B. Stiles, *History of the County of Kings and City of Brooklyn* (New York: W.W. Munsell, 1884).

48. Hall, 118.

49. Ibid., 92.

50. Ibid.

51. Douglas C. North, Terry Anderson and Peter J. Hill, *Growth and Welfare in the American Past, A New Economic History* (Englewood Cliffs: Prentice-Hall, 1983), 103.

52. Hall, 92.

53. Welles and Prios, 16.

54. United States Population Censuses, All Suffolk Towns, 1870, 1880.

55. Welles and Prios, 80-81.

56. Hall, 119.

57. Ibid.

58. Ibid.

59. Ibid.

60. Ibid., 120.

61. *Census of the State of New York for 1875* (Albany: Weed, Parson and Co., 1877), xxxii.

62. Ibid.

63. Ibid.

64. All figures from BCH and Welles and Prios.

65. Hall, 121.

66. Hall, 101.

CHAPTER TWO

The Business of Shipbuilding

Throughout its history wooden shipbuilding retained a very personal business organization that centered around single proprietors or partnerships, the latter usually familial in nature. In this regard, wooden shipbuilding followed eighteenth-century patterns, which survived until circa 1840. The survival of such basic forms of business enterprise was due to the low speed of production and slow seasonal movement of goods through the antebellum American economy. This meant that maximum daily activity at each point of production and distribution in many lines of business could easily be handled by small enterprises owned and managed by one man or one family.[1] Wooden shipbuilding fit this model perfectly. A few years, perhaps seasons, of experience would enable a ship carpenter to set himself up as a master carpenter or "boss"—provided he could raise enough capital and also interest clients in a project. Before 1860, the competition of a hundred different firms kept prices close to production costs, which meant that few fortunes were made in shipbuilding as opposed to commerce. Ease of entry into the business and the resultant heavy competition worked against the appearance of economies of scale in wooden shipbuilding. Before 1857, the older, more experienced yards expanded their capacity to four to six ships at a time. This was the maximum output attainable without encountering serious diseconomies.[2]

With the appearance of massive industrialization during and after the Civil War, more sophisticated means of capitalization, ownership and organization were ushered in. But wooden shipbuilding remained generally unaffected by these developments, retaining its traditional family ownership and management. This was partly a consequence of the diminishing scale of wooden shipbuilding after 1860. It may also have been a result of the trade's continual reliance on the employment of more or fewer workmen as the means of increasing or decreasing production. This pattern was common among all construction trades before 1860. Wooden shipbuilding never faced a real need to adopt more elaborate forms of business organization. In the latter half of the nineteenth century, while corporate organization and separation of ownership and control became the norm in an ever-widening segment of American industry, the shipyards retained the old one- or two-man ownership and management patterns.

The success or failure of a nineteenth-century shipbuilder depended on his skill, energy, marketing ability and—probably—his luck. The shipyard owner, or "boss," bore ultimate responsibility for completing his vessels according to the specifications of the contract. His products were figuratively stamped with his name; their durability and seaworthiness determined his reputation and, consequently, his success. Ordinarily the shipbuilder's reputation was the key to the success of a yard. As a result, it is not surprising that the "boss" oversaw, and sometimes participated in, the construction of a vessel long after financial security removed the direct need to do so. When describing the work habits of James E. Bayles in 1885, the Port Jefferson *Times* reported that "He superintends personally, the laying out of all new vessels in their yard, and seldom entrusts to others the supervision or planning of the delicate work of outlining and setting up his forms."[3]

The construction of wooden ships was a complex operation, and personal supervision at all stages, even when assisted by a seasoned foreman and crew, was both painstaking and time-consuming. It is appropriate here to give an outline of the process of wooden shipbuilding in America in the last century, from the design of a vessel to its launching.

The Shipyard

The first act in the construction of a vessel was the preparation of a carefully carved half model—often made with "lifts," or alternating layers of wood of two contrasting shades. This model of half the hull from bow to stern, with the horizontal bands of its lifts if it was made that way, represented the shape of the hull from any angle. The model was the design of the hull in three dimensions, and its curves and proportions were copied full-size in "lofting" the vessel. The

Caulking

Coppering

The Steam Chest

Interior of the Ship

parts of a lift model could be separated to make possible very accurate full-scale lines laid down in the mold loft. This loft was a large room where the lines of the vessel were drawn or laid down on the floor, and full-size molds or templates were made for every piece of the vessel's frame.

The construction of a vessel began with a keel, normally of white oak, laid on blocks. The frame pieces—stem, ribs, deadwood—were cut to shape following the lines laid down on the lofting floor and then assembled on a platform built over the keel. This platform could be moved fore or aft as needed. The finished frames, also normally of white oak, were then hoisted up on the keel. Frame components were fastened to the keel with substantial spikes and bolts, and most shipyards had their own forges to make these fastenings. When all the

The Launching of the Ship

frames were up, men with adzes carefully dubbed the frames fair to accommodate the planking.

When the framing was completed, long planks of yellow pine were cut with a pit saw and, if necessary, softened for bending in a steam chest. Steambending was more often necessary with oak than with yellow pine or cedar. Planks were bent into place and held by a variety of clamps and wedges. They were then fastened to the skeleton of frames with wooden pegs of locust called treenails (pronounced "trunnels") driven into holes made by an auger. Men with adzes smoothed the planking before and after the caulking process. The caulkers with their mesquite mallets and caulking irons filled the narrow seams between the planks with strands of oakum to help make the hull watertight.

Meanwhile, other shipwrights were inside the ship that was taking shape, installing deck beams and decks, soles (floors), ceilings (inner planking), and much other structure. When the decks and soles were in, the joiners did their work—fashioning cabins and cabinets, hatches and rails, and in general doing the fine work of the vessel, which might include decorative carving. Then the painters and varnishers finished the hull inside and out. After the masts were installed, or "stepped," the riggers took over. Finally—fresh-painted, rigged and equipped, and with flags flying—the new vessel was launched, although many vessels went into the water before being rigged.

It should be mentioned that the half models made in planning a vessel could be used in bidding for a contract. In such a manner James E. Bayles won a contract from J. and W. R. Wing of New Bedford, Massachusetts, to build the 328-ton whaling bark *Fleetwing* in 1877.[4] The design of these vessels, and the carving of the half models, was normally the responsibility of the "boss" builder himself. Such was the case with Bayles and Jesse Carll. Similarly, when he took over Northport operations from his father, Erastus Hartt carved the models and lofted the lines of all his own vessels. Occasionally a shipbuilder would hire someone with a special talent in ship design if it exceeded his own. This was the case with Hiram Ketcham, who did much of the design and modeling for the Greenport builder Oliver Bishop. John T. Mather's partnership with Owen Wood from 1873 to 1903 was founded on Wood's considerable talent as a ship designer.

Although boats and ships were built early in Long Island's history, no builder or area laid deep roots in the trade before the nineteenth century. When permanent shipbuilding centers emerged after the War of 1812, they were characterized by a strong family orientation. With the possible exception of John Willse, none of the men who came to found Suffolk County's yards sprang from a family with shipbuilding experience. After the first nineteenth-century firms were established, however, several of the shipbuilding families developed interconnections, and some general lines of descent in the development and transmission of shipbuilding skills can be traced.

John R. Mather

Nowhere was the interfamilial shipbuilding tradition stronger than in Port Jefferson. (See The Willse Connection, Figure 1, Page 3). Both of the two leading families traced their lineage to John Willse who, as noted above, began production in Port Jefferson in 1799. Richard Mather, and possibly his brother, Titus, were apprenticed to Willse by 1809. Richard subsequently married Willse's daughter, Irena, who bore him a son, John R. Mather. Richard Mather succeeded Willse as the village's most important shipbuilder until his career was cut short by an accident in 1816, after which no vessel was constructed in Drowned Meadow for five years. William L. Jones, who came from what had been described as a "wealthy" Comsewogue family, apprenticed with Titus Mather and went on to marry the widowed Irena Willse Mather in 1821. A dispute with Willse's son John, over use of a dock, probably built by Willse, led Titus Mather to quit Port Jefferson for Bridgeport in 1825.[5] He continued the shipbuilding trade in Connecticut.

Whatever young John R. Mather learned from his stepfather, William L. Jones, he apparently felt his uncle could teach him more, and in 1831 he crossed the Sound to work under Titus in Bridgeport. In 1837, he returned to Port Jefferson and entered a partnership with his stepfather.[6] In 1845, Jones turned over the business to his stepson and his own son, William L. Jones, Jr. The younger Jones retired from the industry in the early 1850s. It seems clear that John R. Mather was the driving force behind the Jones-Mather shipbuilding operation, as all ships launched from the yard after 1838 were built under his name.[7]

In 1809, about the same time that Richard Mather was apprenticing with John Willse, Elisha Bayles of Mount Sinai moved to Port Jefferson and began working as a rigger and caulker. Elisha Bayles was probably another who learned his trade at the Willse yard since his family background had been in shoemak-

Nehemiah Hand

ing, masonry and milling. Bayles worked primarily for other people, although
he built a few vessels on private contract in the 1830s. In 1836 Elisha's two
sons, James M. and C. Lloyd , went into business for themselves, a partnership
that lasted till 1856. C. Lloyd also served three years as a shipbuilding apprentice in the Housatonic River village of Derby, Connecticut. Where he worked in
Derby is not known.[8] James M. Bayles went on to become the most successful
builder in Port Jefferson. While James M. and C. Lloyd. were still partners, two
brothers from Northport arrived in Port Jefferson to learn the craft of shipbuilding from them. These were David and Jesse Carll, who returned to Northport
in 1850 to establish what became Northport's leading shipyard.

The evolutionary thread extending from John Willse to the major shipbuilders of the nineteenth century on Long Island is striking. This interconnec-
tion takes on added significance when one realizes that, with the exception of
Willse, whose pre-Long-Island career is unknown, none of the shipbuilding
families had any training in the trade until Willse himself appeared. Fortunately,
shipbuilding in the eighteenth and early nineteenth century was part of an arti-
san tradition, with hardly any formal education or engineering theory necessary.
On-the-job training, apprenticing under a master ship's carpenter, was the way
the skills of the craft were perpetuated and disseminated. The right geographic
location, presence of a competent ship's carpenter, and market demand were
sufficient to induce some men to attempt a career in shipbuilding. As the nineteenth century wore on, and vessels progressed to greater size and complexity,
the industry became more specialized and more difficult to start up.
Nevertheless, from its beginning until its extinction, wooden shipbuilding—
especially in places like Northport or Port Jefferson—was organized more on
craft than industrial lines.

Northport's second leading shipbuilding firm also had a strong family tradition. The Hartt family, led by brothers Samuel Prior and Moses B., established their shipbuilding operation in the 1830s. The Hartts were natives of Huntington Town and, like the Carll brothers, had no interests in shipbuilding before the 1830s. Where they got their training in shipbuilding is unknown. Nevertheless, they set a family precedent that held good for the rest of the century. Samuel P. was succeeded by his son, Erastus, who in turn was joined by his son, Oliver, as the industry entered its twilight in the 1890s.

The career of Nehemiah Hand, Setauket's major builder, resembles that of the Mathers, Bayleses and Carlls. Hand was a posthumous child, born January 19, 1819, two months after his father's death. The family home was at Fireplace, on the South Shore of Brookhaven Town, although they were probably a branch of the Hand family of East Hampton. Nehemiah's first profession was carpentry. But he did not enjoy the work and, as he later recalled, "In my 17th year I was determined to learn the shipwright's trade and walked eighteen miles to Stony Brook to see my brother who was a shipwright. He agreed to give me my board and clothes and a quarter's schooling till I was twenty-one. The schooling I did not get."[9] Where Silas, Nehemiah's brother, had learned his craft is not clear. Stony Brook remained a secondary shipbuilding center throughout the nineteenth century, and both Hands relocated in Setauket in 1833. Again, the pattern of an important shipbuilder springing from a non-shipbuilding family emerges. Nehemiah's father was a fisherman, and Fireplace never developed into a shipbuilding village. Nehemiah Hand was another part of the Willse-Mather connection. In 1835 he worked for Titus Mather in Bridgeport. A single line in an 1883 news article also indicates that he spent some time in the Mather-Jones yard in Port Jefferson.[10]

Capital Improvements

While the deeply indented North Shore harbors provided excellent natural settings for shipbuilding, it was often necessary for the builders to construct docks and marine railways, or to undertake even more extensive projects to insure the profitability of their enterprises. Sometimes the builders moved within a village, shifting the location of their yards in an attempt to gain a more advantageous site, perhaps with more flat land at the foreshore or deeper water off the beach.

Permission to build docks or wharves was obtained by petition from the town governments, which held jurisdiction over water and underwater developments in their harbors. In 1807, John Willse received permission from Brookhaven Town to build a pier six yards long.[11] Although John Willse constructed this small pier, it and the Willse shipyard ashore were not enough to make Port Jefferson a major shipbuilding village. It was the improvements made by William L. Jones, John R. Mather's stepfather, that shaped Port Jefferson's future. After completing a 500-foot wharf, Jones began an ambitious project to improve the east side of the harbor where his shipyard stood. He then bought much of the adjacent high ground, and he commenced filling in the low areas near the water. He also constructed an elevated road along what is now East Main Street. His development of the east side of the village was so extensive that in 1870 a full 40 percent of Port Jefferson's businesses were reportedly located on land Jones had made available for future use.[12] After his wharf was finished in 1827, Jones began to divert a stream that flowed into the harbor. His completed channel allowed him to float vessels from his yard directly into the harbor at high tide.[13] Lastly, in 1841, Jones installed marine railways for the efficient hauling and launching of ships and boats.

Jones' improvements, while designed to further his shipbuilding activities, proved a boon for Port Jefferson's growth as a village. But it seems these labors of more than four years became a financial disaster for Jones,[14] probably because he was unable to immediately recoup his expenditures. By 1845, Jones had handed his operations over to his son and stepson. What the future of Port Jefferson's shipbuilding industry might have been without Jones' expensive improvements is impossible to estimate. Some credit the growth of the village's output from less than one ship a year during the years 1797 to 1831, to an average of six a year from 1832 to 1884, to these expansions of the shipyard's physical plant.[15] Such a claim on the supply side discounts any gain in production generated by the increasing demand for ships during much of the period. Nevertheless, these improvements at the Mather-Jones yard surely facilitated economic development and, by making the harbor more attractive and accessible to other builders, promoted shipbuilding in the village. An unambiguous sign of Port Jefferson's growing importance as a maritime center was its designation by the United States Congress as an official port of entry in 1852.

About the time Jones was developing the east side of the waterfront, suggestions were made for improving the harbor itself. Nothing came of such proposals until the Rivers and Harbors Act was passed in the United States Congress in 1871. The original legislation provided for the dredging of a channel seven feet deep, 100 feet wide, and extending from the mouth to the foot of the harbor. An 1875 modification of the original bill called for the construction of a jetty on the west side of the harbor entrance. In 1877, funds were voted to extend the area to be dredged to a channel eight feet deep and 200 feet wide. An earthen jetty was to be extended to retard the movement of the sands into the dredged area.[16] Work on these projects proceeded somewhat fitfully, especially when the Grant administration undertook austerity measures, which cut much of the funding. However, by 1883 the channel was 100 feet wide and as much as 18 feet deep at low tide.[17]

As previously noted, in addition to upgrading their facilities, Port Jefferson shipbuilders sometimes changed location in an attempt to gain further advantage. While Jones and Mather were building their new wharves on the village's east side, Matthew Darling and Sylvester Smith, brothers-in-law, had established a business on the site of the old Willse yard. They later moved to the west side of the harbor where they built marine railways and a pier in 1834. Members of the Darling family subsequently set up two shipyards on the west side of the harbor. When James M. and C. Lloyd Bayles began their business in 1836, they chose the old Willse site so recently evacuated by the Darlings.

Despite William L. Jones' improvements, and a deep dredged channel, the Mather-Jones shipyard still lay too far inland for efficiency. Nevertheless, John R. Mather, Jones' stepson and successor, waited 33 years before he relocated to a site just west of the Bayles yard where a marine railway was already in operation. This reluctance to move to a more advantageous spot may have been part of the reason the Mathers failed to retain their position as leading shipbuilders in the village. By the time of the Civil War that distinction had passed to the Bayleses who never lost it. In 1881, when Mather was in partnership with Owen Wood, he installed the first steam-driven marine railway on Long Island. This gave him the capacity to haul vessels of up to 1500 tons.[18]

No other Suffolk shipbuilding port received such extensive improvements as Port Jefferson—and no other Suffolk village proved as successful in the industry. At Northport, construction undertaken to aid the business remained limited to the building of piers and marine railways. The earliest record of a dock/railway system in the Town of Huntington dates to 1844 when Samuel Prior Hartt received a lease from the town "for the purpose of building a dock and railway to repair vessels."[19] The rent was three dollars a year and the term was 15 years, renewable.[20] Three years later, Samuel's brother, Moses Brush Hartt, gained a lease from the town to construct a dock. His rental fee was set at eight dollars and twenty-five cents a year. The higher rent may have been a consequence of the longer lease—21 years.[21] In 1856 the Hartts and Huntington Town entered a protracted dispute over the failure of the Hartts to pay their yearly rent. Why the brothers defaulted on their lease payments is unknown. The modest size of the fee suggests a problem other than financial. Whatever the dispute, between 1856 and 1868 the town repeatedly threatened the Hartts with legal action or sale of their leased property to a third party. In 1868, the Town of Huntington leased Samuel's lot to Charles A. Cheeseborough, who does not seem to have taken possession. Moses Hartt retired shortly after the Civil War, but Samuel continued in the trade until about 1880. His son, Erastus, and his grandson, Oliver, continued as builders into the twentieth century, although the Hartt yard itself was sold by 1890.

In 1855, the Carll brothers, David and Jesse, returned to Northport from their apprenticeship at the Bayles shipyard in Port Jefferson and went into business for themselves. With only $400, which they had inherited from their father's estate as capital, the brothers were forced to purchase land in shoreline strips ten to fifteen feet wide with options to buy more.[22] Despite these early

Jesse Carll

constraints, by 1860 the Carlls operated the largest shipyard in Northport, eclipsing the Hartts who had started earlier. By 1865, the year David left for City Island, the Carll shipyard consisted of 20 acres. This area remained the approximate size of the yard as long as the Carlls owned it.[23] The first lease the Carlls obtained from Huntington Town, on November 15, 1859, included provisions for a marine railway.[24] Jesse Carll later added another set of railways which, his business card boasted, could haul out vessels of 500 tons.[25] Altogether, in 1874 Northport had five sets of marine railways in operation.[26] In comparison with the improvements and facilities at Port Jefferson, Northport's attainments were modest. But they were in keeping with the shipbuilding and repair business of the area, and in 1874 they were enough for Northport to be called the most flourishing village in the Town of Huntington.[27]

After apprenticing with his brother, and gaining experience at Port Jefferson and with the Bell and Brown shipyard in New York City, Nehemiah Hand established his own business at Setauket in 1846. "I found I must make money faster to support my family," he recollected, "so I laid down the first set of [marine rail]ways in Setauket for repairs. Many said all they could against it, and I have found from long experience that it is the character of old settlers generally to oppose all improvements."[28] Hand's yard and railways swiftly became the most important in Setauket. The precise nature of shipbuilding facilities in Greenport at this time is not clear, although marine railways are depicted in illustrations dating from the 1840s.

Peripateticism Among Shipbuilders

Before they succeeded in establishing themselves, shipbuilders sometimes moved around seeking work. In 1835, for example, Moses B. Hartt, later to become an important Northport builder, constructed several "large vessels" on

James M. Bayles

the west side of the Nisseqougue River in Smithtown.[29] Nehemiah Hand, who became Setauket's leading shipbuilder, worked on vessels in several villages, including Port Jefferson, and spent time in a large shipyard in New York City before setting himself up in Setauket. In 1843, Nehemiah's older brother, Silas, under whom he was then apprenticed, sent him to Northport where, as he later testified, he was to "take charge of a gang of men and finish a vessel which I did and launched her."[30] Hand also reported that he built a "small vessel" in Glen Cove.[31] Three years later, tired of working for others, Hand opened his own shipyard. Nehemiah Hand became so successful that he never again had to travel to find work.

Interestingly, Silas Hand, who preceded his brother in the trade, never succeeded in establishing himself permanently in a particular village. His movements between 1840 and 1850 are uncertain. In the latter year he was building ships in Southold Town, probably in Greenport. In 1860 he was in Port Jefferson, and in 1866 he built a ship in Greenport. He was listed as a ship carpenter in Brookhaven Town in the 1870 census, but his last recorded vessel was laid down at Bellport on the South Shore in 1876.[32] Silas came to rest in the Cedar Hill cemetery in Port Jefferson. It is not known if he ever worked for his increasingly prosperous brother. It is clear that Nehemiah never took him into the firm as a partner, and Silas' movements suggest estrangement between the brothers.

Success did not necessarily preclude work outside a shipbuilder's resident village. At least once, James M. Bayles, who founded Port Jefferson's most important shipyard, went to a neighboring community to aid a fellow builder. In 1855, Samuel Carman, a builder active in Stony Brook before the Civil War, asked Bayles' help in lofting the lines and frames of a vessel. According to James E. Bayles, James M.'s son and successor, "Mr. Carman was not a practical builder. I remember he came to my father to make the model for the *Tanner* and afterwards father 'laid it down' and furnished the moulds or patterns for the frames, etc."[33] It should be noted that this event took place early in Bayles' career, and that he never seems to have taken such an assignment again.

Hiram Bishop, an active builder in Greenport from 1839 to 1855, was as peripatetic as the Hands. In addition to building 32 ships in Greenport during those years, he also constructed two schooners and three sloops at Moriches, two sloops at Speonk, a sloop and a schooner at Squier's Landing (Peconic), and a sloop at Wading River.[34] Apparently, Bishop went wherever he could get a contract. His movements suggest that contracting parties could insist that second-level builders construct their vessels at the contractor's village. Silas Hand's career supports the premise that shipbuilders who failed to establish a successful yard had to follow the work. Consequently, the lives of second-level shipbuilders sometimes resembled those of the ship carpenters, caulkers, riggers and other members of the industry's labor force rather than that of the established master builders. In this regard, the nineteenth-century shipbuilding industry parallels the contemporary aerospace industry whose workers, in all but the highest levels, move about the country seeking employment with those firms that have current contracts.

The most interesting case of a Long Island builder working outside his village concerns Northport shipbuilder Nathaniel R. White. In April of 1870 White received a commission to build a schooner in Maine.[35] This curious arrangement suggests that the contractor, Captain James Velsor, chose a Maine shipyard for its lower costs but admired White's products so much that he tapped him for the design and construction. Another Long Island shipwright, Hiram Bishop, who frequently worked as designer for Greenport builder Oliver Bishop, received a contract to supply the half-model and moulds for a 200-ton schooner to be built at Bath, Maine.[36] In this instance the shipbuilder did not go to the work, the work came to the shipbuilder.

The Nature of Business Partnerships

The essential family orientation of Long Island shipbuilding has already been noted. Especially before 1870, even the composition of family firms was fluid, and partnerships were made and broken with speed and ease. In this, shipbuilding resembled house building and other undercapitalized small-scale industries in the nineteenth century and in our own time. Partnerships in shipbuilding were most common between 1850 and 1870. This phenomenon owed something to the increasing cost of vessels and a concomitant rise in capital requirements. It may also have reflected a growing division of labor in which one partner served as business manager while the other functioned as designer/engineer or naval architect.[37]

On Long Island the proliferation of partnerships is best illustrated by the careers of the Darling family. At least six members of this family came to Port Jefferson during the 1830s: Matthew, Brewster, John L., Charles, William and Jeremiah. Of these six, three—Matthew, Charles and Jeremiah—built ships under their own names or in partnerships. The combined Darling output was the greatest in Port Jefferson during the 1830s.[38]

In 1832, Matthew Darling began a partnership with his brother-in-law, Sylvester Smith, and the two opened a shipyard on the old Willse grounds. One year later they relocated to the west side of the harbor, which remained the focal point of Darling activity until the 1870s. The firm of Smith and Darling lasted until 1840 when the two men parted company. However, Smith built one vessel with Jeremiah Darling in 1846. Charles and Jeremiah Darling turned out vessels together in the late 1840s, and they also took contracts separately. At approximately the same time, William Darling formed a company with Ahira Hawkins which lasted until 1852. Hawkins then teamed up with yet another Darling, John L., in a partnership which only survived until 1854. In the 1850s, Jeremiah Darling formed a partnership with Edward Bedell, then worked on his own from 1857 to 1859, and was a partner with Sylvester Wines in 1860. Wines himself was briefly allied with C. Lloyd Bayles in 1863-64.[39]

The Darlings may have won the prize for the largest number of partnerships among Suffolk County shipbuilders—but their pattern was not unique. The rapidity with which their partnerships were formed and dissolved, coupled with the short-lived nature of many of these combinations, suggests a tremendous desire to succeed and break into the small circle of top-ranked builders. These partnerships seem also to indicate difficulties in raising and maintaining capital, and may well represent a tactic for reducing the burden of overhead. The Darlings never did become major Long Island builders. Despite their numbers, or because of them, the Darlings barely lasted into the 1870s. Matthew Darling's son, Emmet, seems to have been the only member of the family to build ships after the Civil War.[40] In 1865, he allied himself with a local ship designer, Owen Wood. Their partnership lasted until Darling went out of business about 1879. Wood later joined John T. Mather.

While the two leading Port Jefferson shipbuilding families, Bayles and Mather, showed more stability and durability, the Bayleses were capable of intra-family competition. In 1836, James M. and C. Lloyd Bayles took over the shipyard established by their father. Their partnership lasted until 1861, but it did not preclude independent enterprise. James. M. was constructing ships under his own name by 1854 with C. Lloyd following suit in 1855.[41] The commencement of these individual undertakings presaged the dissolution of their partnership six years later. While James M. continually expanded his share of the village's shipbuilding business, C. Lloyd never became more than a minor practitioner, with 20 ships to his credit between 1855 and 1874, when he dropped out of the business entirely.[42] Family tradition holds that, when he made what he deemed to be enough money, "Uncle Lloyd" simply retired.

On occasion sibling rivalry destroyed a family partnership. The very different careers of Silas and Nehemiah Hand are a case in point. More dramatically, after ten years of a successful business partnership, David and Jesse Carll fell into a bitter dispute in 1865. Local tradition maintains that their disagreement degenerated into a fist fight. In the aftermath David left Northport and established his own operation at City Island.

Outlays and Ownerships

The docks and marine railways were only part of the visible fixed capital outlay the builders had to assume. Property taxes also had to be taken into account. Lumber, iron work, cordage, paint, finished goods such as wheels and steering gear, windlasses and sails were just part of the components essential for ship construction. Then there was the cost of the laborers. An itemized example of the costs of a ship's construction is found in the records of Daniel Y. Williamson, a small-scale Stony Brook builder. At right is his complete account, in current dollars, for the building of the 108-ton schooner *Jonas Smith*, a vessel named for another Stony Brook shipbuilder, in 1859.

The $17, 285.22 total for the *Jonas Smith* project was high for such a small vessel. In 1877, James M. Bayles built the 328-ton whaling bark *Fleetwing* for $14,814.96. It should be borne in mind that none of these expenses takes any account of overhead costs. These would include yard maintenance, land taxes, possibly insurance on the yard and the vessel under construction, and vessel registration fees.

Shipbuilders frequently assumed a partial ownership in their vessels. This may have been done to keep competitive costs down, although speculation played a role as well. Records of costs and ownership are spotty. Jesse Carll publicly revealed little of his costs and investment interests. One of his earlier ships, built when he was still in partnership with his brother, David, was a 65-ton double-deck bark called *Storm Bird*. She was built for $35,000, a large sum for such a small vessel.[44] A 450-ton vessel named *Joseph Rudd*, launched in 1871, actually cost less—$34,000. In only seven cases are Carll's interests in his ships known. One was a 449-ton schooner called *Allie R. Chester* that he admitted building for his "own account." In another case he is described simply as a partner. In the remaining instances he was reported as holding one-quarter interest in two vessels, and one-eighth and five-sixteenths in the remainder.[45] Occasionally, Carll might buy a vessel outright. In February of 1871 he purchased the schooner *Annie E. Carll* and the brig *Osseo* from the estate of Carll Valentine. Both ships were products of his own yard. Whether he retained sole ownership is unknown.[46]

The Bayleses also followed the practice of retaining part-ownership of some of their vessels. Early in their careers, James M. and C. Lloyd Bayles may have

timber	$3,187.58
planking	3,559.67
lumber	206.45
iron	429.88
spikes	42.47
cutting, carting, onloading timber	165.41
forelocks	28.44
freight	537.89
grind stone	4.62
gold leaf	10.00
paint	21.80
launching tallow	8.58
windlass and purchase	100.00
steering wheel	20.00
pumps and deadeyes	56.00
scupper lead	4.25
rendered from J. Smith	2,245.84
carpenter work	6,475.00
smith work	437.44
sundries	13.54
iron	21.00
sign	9.36
Total	$17,585.22
Less material left	300.00
Net	$17,285.22[43]

done this from necessity. An 1883 recounting of their partnership recalls that "together they would put up a small sloop for themselves, and perhaps if business was dull would make a voyage or two in her, and then selling out, go to work on another craft."[47] This reminiscence also indicates that the Bayleses dabbled in coasting while they were beginning their careers. Later ownership by the Bayles brothers was probably due to investment rather than necessity. Between 1880 and 1890 they owned shares in 50 to 60 vessels of all types in all trades.[48]

The most complete account of vessel costs and partial ownership was provided by Nehemiah Hand of Setauket. Table 2-1 is Hand's list of ships constructed between 1836 and 1878, when he handed the business over to his son, George N. Hand, his partner since 1863.

An analysis of these vessels yields several conclusions. Hand's evolution as a specialist in ships of increasing size becomes apparent. Of the 21 ships finished between 1836 and 1860, when depression brought the great age of American shipbuilding to an end, three were barks, two were brigs—both larger, deepwater, and partially square-rigged vessels—while 11 were schooners and five were sloops—smaller vessels intended generally for coasting. It is noteworthy that the larger, square-rigged types were not laid down until Hand's second decade as a builder with his own yard. Of the ten vessels he built between 1862 and 1878, three were barks, five were brigs, and one was a brigantine—again, relatively large vessels for Long Island. Only two schooners left his ways during this peri-

Year	Name	Type	Tonnage
1836	*Delight*	schooner	41
1837	*Eliza Jayne*	sloop	35
1839	*Hardscrabble*	sloop	74
1841	*Helen Jayne*	sloop	43
1843	*Dart*	sloop	18
1844	*Commerce*	sloop	84
1845	*Nancy Mills*	schooner	109
1847	*Mary A. Rowland*	schooner	35
1847	*Albemarle*	schooner	154
1848	*South Hampton*	schooner	180
1849	*Marietta Hand*	schooner	137
1850	*Nassau*	schooner	169
1851	*N.Hand*	brig	263
1852	*Chase*	schooner	181
1853	*Flying Eagle*	schooner	182
1854	*C.W.Poultney*	bark	487
1855	*T.W.Rowland*	brig	471
1856	*Urania*	bark	405
1857	*Andromeda*	schooner	261
1859	*Palace*	bark	368
1860	*Aldebaran*	schooner	180

Total vessels: 21 (5 sloops, 11 schooners, 3 barks, and 2 brigs); Total tonnage, 3,977

1862	*Mary E. Rowland*	brig	280
1864	*Americus*	brig	498
1868	*Mary E. Thayer*	brig	272
1870	*Dezaldo*	bark	492
1871	*Daisy*	brig	476
1872	*Thomas Brooks*	barkentine	460
1873	*N.Hand*	schooner	191
1875	*Ferris Thompson*	bark	500
1877	*Irene*	brig	475
1878	*Lottie Moore*	bark	933
1879	*Georgette Lawrence*	schooner	—

Total vessels: 11 (2 schooners, 5 brigs, 3 barks, and 1 barkentine);Total tonnage, 4,577

Source: "Shipbuilding And Tonnage," *Bi-Centennial History of Suffolk County* (Babylon: Budget Steam Print, 1885), 120.

TABLE 2-1
Nehemiah Hand's Account of His Output

od. Aggregate 1836-1860 tonnage stood at 3977, while his 1862-1878 total was 4577. Hand's increased production of larger vessels was not unique. Contemporary observers and researchers have noted the trend toward fewer shipyards, engaged in building larger ships, following the Civil War.

Hand revealed to Richard M. Bayles that he owned shares in nearly 50 percent of his output. He assigned part ownership and command of two of them to his son, Robert N. Apparently this gesture was Hand's way of providing his progeny with a little push in life. As previously noted, Hand's other son, George, was taken into partnership and assumed full control of his father's shipbuilding operation in 1873. Hand built four vessels on his own account—that is, for his sole use or investment. In three instances he later sold part ownerships to sea captains, probably those who commanded them. The number of vessels he identified as built for his own account may well be an underestimation since it is not always clear at what point division of ownership was made. At his death in 1895, Hand held part ownership in four ships. He controlled a one-eighth interest in three vessels and one-sixteenth of the other.[49]

Hand built for his own account not only to reduce price or increase confidence in his work—the latter hardly necessary after 1850—but to share the not-insignificant profits to be made. He candidly revealed the profits made from several of his ventures, but for some of these ships he does not explain what his shares of the profits were. For example, it cannot be determined how well he benefitted from the $45,000 made by the schooner *Georgette Lawrence*. Similarly, while Hand explains that the bark *Dezaldo* paid back her $40,000 in cost in five years, we do not know how long she continued in trade and what Hand realized in net profit. From the tone of Hand's account, and judging from the accompanying fragmentary figures, a healthy profit for the builder/part-owner of these vessels seems the most likely conclusion. Indeed, Hand went out of his way to detail one unsatisfactory experience. This concerned the small brig *Mary E. Thayer*, which the builder described as a "bad luck ship." She was dismasted twice and robbed in Lisbon. Although he does not divulge his share in her, Hand ruefully admitted that she cost him "$2117 for a collision where the captain came across the Atlantic without any lights."[50]

One other significant fact gleaned from Hand's shipbuilding reminiscence is that his prices remained stable throughout his career. The bark *C. W. Poultney*, 487 tons, which he built in 1854, cost $39,000. In 1870 he built a bark named *Dezaldo*, only slightly larger at 492 tons. Her cost was $40,000.[51] Since consumer prices rose approximately 36 percent between 1855 and 1870, Hand's real costs, and ultimately his prices, were actually less in 1870 than in 1855.[52] If Hand's prices were typical of Suffolk County it helps explain how the Long Island builders remained in business after the Civil War while those in Manhattan, hurt by rising labor costs, folded.

Although new-vessel construction, especially with part-ownership, proved lucrative to the Suffolk builders, repair work contributed heavily to their incomes. Their profits from repairs are difficult to ascertain since few records are known to have survived. Nevertheless, all the important builders possessed

Allie R. Chester, *a large cargo schooner, shown during her construction in the Jesse Carll yard in 1883.*

Allie R. Chester *nearly ready for launching.*

Name	Length of Time Owned	Profit Earned	Profit At Sale	Sale Price
Mary Hand	4 years	7,200		
N. Hand	4 years	22,502		
Flying Eagle	?	5,000 (in one trip)		
Mary E. Rowan	Costs in 4 years"at profit"			
Georgette Lawrence	?	45,000		
Dezaldo	?	Paid costs in 5 years		
Daisy	Owner got 10,000 in ? years			

Source: *Munsell's History of Suffolk County*

TABLE 2-2
Nehemiah Hand's Profits from His Vessels

at least one set of marine railways, and these were kept busy hauling ships out of the water for repairs, recaulking, and repainting. Repairs themselves covered an enormous range of activity from a simple coat of bottom paint to refastening sprung planks to rebuilding an entire ship.

Ship repair greatly helped Nehemiah Hand establish himself. In 1846 he built one ship, the schooner *Nancy Mills,* yet he happily remembered he had "all the repairing I could do" and employed 29 men.[53] Repairs also accounted for a large amount of work done by Jesse Carll from the 1860s on. In 1883 he complained that there wasn't enough profit in new-vessel construction. In Munsell's *Suffolk County,* Richard M. Bayles recounted that "finding the margin of profit small on new vessels he [Carll] has, for the past twenty years, sought to do only enough to keep his men steadily employed."[54] (See Chapter Six, page 116, for a further discussion of ship repair.)

Shipbuilding, even without business fluctuations, could be a volatile industry. Ships constructed on the builder's own account might not earn a profit, and contractors might default. *Storm Bird,* the third ship launched by David and Jesse Carll, was a 680-ton double-deck bark built for a southerner named Appleton Oak Smith. Her construction cost was $35,000, but the brothers turned her over to Smith before receiving full payment. Smith reneged and the Carlls lost $7000 on the contract. Although this left them $4000 in debt, they were able to recoup this and other losses to such an extent that when they dissolved their partnership in 1855 they split assets of $50,000.[55]

Nehemiah Hand faced a similar problem in 1859. He constructed a bark, *Palace,* for parties who, for obscure reasons, refused to pay the builder's $24,000 fee despite the fact that he had finished her three days ahead of schedule. However, Hand was able to retain the legal services of Samuel Tilden, who succeeded in getting him paid in full.[56] Such difficulties in collecting debt may have contributed to the practice, which dates to the colonial period, of using installment payments for vessels. With this system, a certain percentage of the total price fell due as different stages of the ship were completed. On October

The bark Carib *under construction in the Bayles shipyard in 1868.*

29, 1863, Samuel P. Hartt contracted to build a sloop of not less than 51 tons. The full price was set at $3060, but Hartt was to be paid in installments as the vessel progressed.[57] Similarly, in December of 1864, James M. Bayles signed an agreement with Rodney Parker of Chester, Connecticut, to build a sloop at $62 a ton. The contract specified that one-fifth of the cost would be paid when the keel was laid, one-fifth when the frame was raised, one-fifth when the vessel in frame was ceilinged and nailed, one-fifth when planked, and one-fifth when it was launched.[58] In addition to insuring that the builder did not assume uncollectible construction costs, installment payments may have made new ships more readily affordable by owners.

The Civil War had a depressing effect on United States sea trade, and thus on demand for vessels, as Confederate commerce raiders made sailing under the American flag hazardous and expensive. Nehemiah Hand felt the impact of Confederate naval activities directly. In 1860, Hand launched the schooner *Aldebaran,* and turned over one-eighth interest plus command to his son, Robert. On March 13, 1863, the schooner was captured by the Confederate raider *Florida.* Robert and his crew were taken from the schooner and sent to Scotland. Almost immediately, Hand filed a claim for *Aldebaran's* value in Washington. Thirteen years later, after the settlement of the "Alabama Claims,"

Hand received $30,160 plus four-percent interest to cover the loss of the ship.[59] This seems to have been a generous settlement, even considering the loss of *Aldebaran's* possible profits over 13 years.

Hand eventually landed on his feet in the *Aldebaran-Florida* affair. Other builders could not survive such losses, or the shipping depression caused by the war. Although no other builder on Long Island seems to have been hurt so

The whaling brig Daisy, *built in 1872 by Nehemiah and George Hand, and active as a whaler and cargo-carrier until 1916.*

directly by the Civil War as Nehemiah Hand, there were other ways a ship-builder could be ruined. One such road to financial disaster was misjudging the market for new vessels. Such a mistake ruined the career of David B. Bayles of Setauket, who turned out 16 ships between 1847 and 1869.[60] Although only a second-level builder, Bayles constructed what was probably the largest sailing ship ever launched on Long Island, the 1460-ton *Adorna*.[61] A few years later, he began work on an even larger vessel. Known locally as "the big ship," this capacious new project's dimensions were 240 feet in length, 47 feet in beam and 34 feet in depth.[62]

Although Bayles himself seems to have invested in the ship, the work was contracted for and underwritten by a "Captain Davis" who was engaged in the cotton trade. Work had to be halted before the ship was completed when Davis suffered financial distress and defaulted on the contract.[63] Finally, in 1876, the ship was completed as something other than intended and launched as a steam-propelled coal barge named *Wilkes-Barre*. Even in this diminished and disgraced condition, the "big ship" was a large cargo-carrier measured at 3700 tons.[64]

The effect of this fiasco on Bayles, now an elderly man, was dramatic. On July 26, 1870, the agent for R.G. Dun and Company wrote that Bayles "failed about five years ago. Is an honest straightforward man but considered in debt...Is worthy of small cr[edit] (yet we can't warrant it)."[65] The date of the

The 500-ton bark Ferris Thompson, *built by the Hands in 1875.*

report suggests that Bayles had trouble with the *Adorna* project, or immediately upon beginning the "big ship." The R.G. Dun and Company report of February 6, 1873, was even more gloomy. Bayles, it states, was an "old man aged 70 with but little and don't do much[;] just about manages to live."[66] David Bayles appears in the R.G. Dun and Company reports for the last time on February 26, 1878. After mentioning that he had failed "some years ago," the agent continued that his "wife secured title to the homestead...[he] is employed by the day now."[67]

New York City Connections

Suffolk County shipbuilders benefitted greatly from their proximity to New York City. The great port generated demand for ships, some of them Long-Island built, and its store of supplies and technology were frequently a resource for the Island's builders. A dependency on New York for maritime supplies not manufactured locally dates to the infancy of the Island's shipbuilding industry. In 1807, an unidentified Stony Brook builder laying down the sloop *Woodcock* sent to Schermerhorn's chandlery in New York for tar and turpentine.[68] Another unidentified builder working in the Stony Brook-Setauket area in the 1820s similarly recorded sending to New York for spars and iron for a sloop called *Ohio*.[69] A decade later, Jonas Smith of Stony Brook was outfitting his ships with the aid of South Street ship chandleries, and his lumber was acquired from Campbell and Moody, situated on Manhattan's Hudson River waterfront.[70] David B. Bayles of Setauket dealt with both Greenpoint and South Street merchants for such basic items as spikes and bolts.[71]

This reliance on New York nautical supplies was not confined to Stony Brook-Setauket builders in the antebellum period. The ship chandlery firm of Whitlock and Glover, located at 57 South Street, found it useful to advertise in the Port Jefferson *Times* during the 1880s.[72] It is likely that all of Suffolk's builders relied on New York City for much of their hardware and such sophisticated items as compasses. Nor were they alone. Even so successful a shipbuilding and shipping-line family as the Mallorys of Mystic, Connecticut, made regular trips to New York to purchase gear and supplies not made or available locally. It is likely that shipbuilders in peripheral areas depended on the nearby commercial centers to supply many items essential for their business.

New York City's importance to the Suffolk builders extended beyond its role as a purveyor of nautical necessities. The great city of shipping and shipbuilding was a purveyor of skills. Nehemiah Hand learned the techniques of square-rigged ship construction in New York yards in 1838. The Bell and Brown shipyard provided work for Hand again in 1842 when "business was very dull and I worked...by the day."[73]

New York's financial houses also served as a source of capital to the Island's shipbuilders, since none of the shipbuilding villages had banking institutions

until late in the nineteenth century. Some New York investment firms contracted with Long Island builders for vessels they needed for their commercial interests, as well as for general investment purposes by means of part-ownership. In
such a way the New York commercial and investment firm of Woodhouse and
Rudd acted as bankers and backers for the Carll shipyard in Northport. By
1882, Jesse Carll and Joseph Rudd had formed some sort of partnership. Such a
connection gave Carll access to the rarefied financial markets of the City, and
Carll proudly listed Woodhouse and Rudd, capitalized at $150-$175,000 in
1868,[74] as references on his business cards.

Diversification

Considering the vulnerability of their industry to economic downturns and
prevailing market conditions, it is not surprising that the Suffolk shipbuilders
sought to diversify their business interests and pursue other sources of capital.
Ship chandleries, stores dealing in the furnishings necessary to outfit a vessel,
were logical areas for business investment, and several builders pursued this line.
The most durable and important of these chandleries was that run by the
Bayleses in Port Jefferson. This enterprise had its beginnings in the grocery store
opened by Elisha Bayles during the time he was presumably working at the
John Willse yard. When Elisha's sons, James M. and C. Lloyd Bayles, began
their operations in the 1840s, they inherited the chandlery as well. James M.
continued this branch of the family business after breaking with his brother and
expanded it into a general merchandise store. His son, George F., took over its
operation when his other son, James Elbert, assumed control of the shipyard.[75]
The store was already an asset in the 1850s when R.G. Dun and Company
agents estimated the net value of the partners at $3000, with their real-estate
holdings estimated at $2000.[76] The Bayles family's general-store activities were
not unique. An unidentified Stony Brook or Setauket shipbuilder had run a
general store along with a shipyard during the 1820-1840 period. Indeed, after
1826 his accounts relate entirely to general merchandising.[77]

John R. Mather was also engaged in mercantile activities ashore. By 1863, if
not before, he was in business with Frederick J. Darling and William M. Jones
in a combination general store and lumber business. In 1873, Mather and
Darling split, Darling taking the store and Mather the lumber business. Mather
was reportedly worth $50,000 at this point, although the figure probably
includes income from his shipyard as well.[78] Mather was still in the lumber business (which was a good way to beat middlemens' costs for his ship lumber) in
1888. At this point he was in partnership with William M. Jones, son of
William L., who was reported to have other business interests in Brooklyn. The
last R.G. Dun and Company report concerning this combination states that
they were "doing a prosperous business" with an estimated worth, apparently

The Bayles store in 1895.

combined, of $60-70,000.[79] The latter figure clearly excludes any of Mather's assets from his shipbuilding. Another builder who engaged in the lumber business was David T. Bayles, a minor Stony Brook builder. He had abandoned shipbuilding for lumber entirely by the 1880s and became prominent enough to get involved in the Smithtown and Port Jefferson Railroad scheme with Nehemiah Hand and the Port Jefferson Byleses.

Real estate seems to have been another attractive investment for some Suffolk builders. R.G. Dun and Company agents made brief reports of sizable real-estate investments by Nehemiah Hand and the Byleses. Unfortunately, they did not give the size and location of real-estate holdings other than the builders' homes and shipyards.[80] Jesse Carll was reputed to possess extensive landholdings in South Dakota.[81] At least one shipbuilder, Emmet B. Darling, tried farming, probably because of declining shipbuilding work in the 1870s. This venture proved unsuccessful and he leased his land and auctioned off his stock and farm implements in March of 1880.[82]

As noted above, both Nehemiah Hand and James M. Bayles became involved in Long Island railroad development. In 1861-62, the shipbuilders had joined Carll S. Burr, Joel Smith and a "Mr. Shipman" to form the Smithtown and Port Jefferson Railroad. In 1870, James M. Bayles became the president and Hand one of the directors of the line. Their investment company raised $85,000, secured the right of way, and commenced building the railroad.[83] Apparently they always envisioned their line being absorbed by the Long Island Railroad. Bayles and his Board of Directors negotiated with Charles Charlick,

President of the Long Island Railroad, to get that company to guarantee the Smithtown and Port Jefferson's bonds. The line was completed as planned in 1873. James E. Bayles later became a director of the line, serving on the Board until it became part of the Long Island Railroad system. Today the Smithtown and Port Jefferson survives as the eastern end of the Long Island's Port Jefferson branch.

What the original group of investors realized from their railroad speculation, if anything, is not known. Neither the census evaluations nor the R.G. Dun reports give any indication of financial losses. Without doubt, the shipbuilders' railroad program played an important role in opening north-central Suffolk to development. Paradoxically, the opening of the area to the railroad may have reduced the volume of freight being shipped on Port Jefferson's schooners and sloops. It certainly contributed to the demise of the Long Island Steamship Company.

Suffolk County shipbuilders seemed well-disposed toward any enterprises with moneymaking potential. Indeed, the general impression is one of Yankee shrewdness—although this opportunism, part of our folklore, guaranteed nothing. Not all investments were preordained towards success, and some seem to have come to nothing. Such appears to have been the fate of a sand-mining operation partly owned by David and Jesse Carll in 1859.[84] Nehemiah Hand seems never to have let a money-making opportunity pass. During a visit to Albany in 1865 he found ashes selling at twelve and one-half cents a bushel. Realizing he could sell them at twice that price on Long Island, Hand bought all he could in Albany and other towns in the Hudson River Valley, returned to Long Island and sold them at twenty-four to twenty-five cents a bushel. According to his own account, he then "bought and sold some gold and anything else I could make money on."[85] Hand's ashes arbitrage and the buying and selling of "anything else I could make money on" seems a compulsive, almost miserly, maneuver. Nothing quite like it has survived in the record regarding any other builder. Yet Hand was obviously proud of the business acumen he demonstrated and related the whole tale to Richard M. Bayles who included it in *Munsell's History of Suffolk County.* It may be that Hand's insecure start in life, combined with a naturally flinty nature, induced a mania for money-making. How this appeared to members of his own community may be gauged by the following doggerel composed and recited in 19th-century Setauket: "Nehemiah, Trustee buyer, Thief on sea and land, When the devil gets you 'miah, He'll have a job on Hand!"

One of the most important steps any town or village could undertake to facilitate economic development was the founding of a bank to provide a source of loan and short-term investment capital sensitive to local requirements. James E. Bayles was a prime mover in the establishment of the Bank of Port Jefferson in June of 1889. He served as one of the bank's directors and as first vice-president until December 11, 1924, when he became president. At the time of his death in 1927 the bank held assets of $1,787,211.50.[86] Similarly, Jesse Carll played a role in founding the Bank of Huntington, and served on its board of directors until his death in 1902. While Nehemiah Hand did nothing to aid the establishment of a bank in the Setauket area, he is known to have personally provided one of banking's most important functions: lending money. Upon his death on November 19, 1894, five notes due him were outstanding. The total of principal and interest was $1871.99. Hand charged his debtors six-percent interest.[87]

Notes:

1. Alfred D. Chandler, Jr. *The Visible Hand, The Managerial Revolution in American Business* (Cambridge, Mass: Harvard University Press, 1977), 15.

2. John G.B. Hutchins, *The American Maritime Industries and Public Policy, 1789-1914* (Cambridge, Mass: Harvard University Press, 1941), 275.

3. Port Jefferson *Times,* 1885. Clipping, Bayles Scrapbook, Frances Child Collection.

4. J. and W.R. Wing to James E. Bayles, September, 1877. Mss. FCC.

5. Gordon Welles and William Prios, *Port Jefferson, Story of a Village* (Port Jefferson: Historical Society of Greater Port Jefferson, 1977) 9-10.

6. Richard M. Bayles "Brookhaven" in *Munsell's History of Suffolk County* (New York: W.W. Munsell and Co., 1883), 83.

7. Welles and Prios, 15.

8. PJT, November 30, 1901, 3.

9. Bayles in Munsell, 84

10. PJT, November 10, 1883, 3.

11. Welles and Prios, 8.

12. Ibid., 10-11.

13. Ibid.

14. Ibid., 22.

15. Ibid., 11.

16. Ibid., 11.

17. Ibid., 19.

18. Ibid., 15.

19. Charles R. Street (compiler), *Huntington Town Records, 1653-1887,* III. (Huntington: 1889), 389.

20. Ibid.

21. Ibid., 396.

22. Recorded interview with Jesse Carll III. No date, c. 1970. Northport Public Library.

23. Huntington Tax Assessments, 1860-1900. Town Historian's Office and Town Recorder's Office.

24. HTR, III, 450.

25. Business card, Jesse Carll, c. 1890, Northport Historical Society.

26. Richard M. Bayles, *Historical and Descriptive Sketches of Suffolk County* (Port Jefferson, 1874), 103.

27. Ibid.

28. Bayles in Munsell, 85.

29. Shipbuilding Folder. Norman O'Berry Collection, Mss. Local History Room, Smithtown Public Library.

30. Bayles in Munsell, 84.

31. Ibid.

32. *Bi-Centennial History of Suffolk County,* (Babylon: Budget Steam Print, 1885), 125.

33. Henry B. Sleight (ed.) *Town Records of the Town of Smithtown,* Vol. I., (Smithtown, 1929), 296.

34. BCH, 125.

35. *Republican Watchman* (Greenport), April 9, 1870, 3.

36. Ibid., August 13, 1870, 3.

37. Hutchins, 275.

38. Welles and Prios, 13.

39. Ibid., 14-15, BCH, 110-114.

40. Welles and Prios, 15.

41. BCH, 111-112.

42. Ibid.

43. Daniel Y. Williamson Papers. Mss. Museums at Stony Brook.

44. Charles R. Street, "Huntington" in Munsell, 37.

45. Ibid.

46. *Republican Watchman,* February 4, 1871, 3.

47. PJT, October 13, 1883, 3.

48. Ibid.

49. Administration papers of the estate of Nehemiah Hand. March 12, 1895. Suffolk County Surrogate's Court. File 13014.

50. Bayles in Munsell, 86.

51. Ibid., 85-86.

52. Consumer Price Index, 1800-1900, United States Department of Commerce, Bureau of Labor Statistics, *Historical Statistics of the United States,* 1790-1970. Vol. I, (Washington, DC: 1975), 210-211.

53. Bayles in Munsell, 186

54. Ibid., 110.

55. Ibid., 87.

56. Ibid., 85.

57. Contract, Samuel P. Hartt with Captain William Hamilton and Samuel S. Brown, October 29, 1863. Mss. Huntington Historical Society.

58. Contract, James M. Bayles with Rodney Parker, December 1864. Mss. Frank & Frances Child Collection.

59. Bayles in Munsell, 47.

60. BCH, 120.

61. William Minuse, Shipbuilding in Setauket. Mimeographed, 1955, 5.

62. Ibid.

63. Ibid.

64. BCH, 58.

65. Records of R.G. Dun & Company Collection. New York, Vol 548, p. 396. Baker Library, Harvard Graduate School of Business Administration.

66. Ibid.

67. Ibid.

68. Vessel Book, Sloop *Woodcock*, 1807-10. Mss. Three Village Historical Society.

69. Ledger, 1820-47, unknown shipbuilder-merchant. Mss. 3VHS

70. Daniel Y. Williamson Papers. Folder 3. Mss. SCMSB.

71. David B. Bayles Ledger, 1854-57. Mss. 3VHS.

72. PJT, February 21, 1880, 4.

73. Bayles in Munsell, 185.

74. R.G. Dun and Company Collection, New York, Vol. 348, p. 858.

75. Bayles in Munsell, 61.

76. R.G. Dun & Company Collection, New York, Vol. 582, p. 53.

77. Ledger, 1820-1847, unknown builder-merchant, Mss. 3VHS.

78. R.G. Dun & Company, New York, Vol. 582, p. 51 and New York, Vol. 584, p. 392.

79. Ibid. New York Vol. 585, p. 893.

80. Ibid. New York, Vol. 584, p. 396 and New York Vol. 585, p. 78.

81. Gay Wagner, *History of Bayview Avenue,* 8.

82. PJT, March 13, 1880, 3.

83. Bayles in Munsell, 86. In the early 1860s, several Port Jefferson residents formed the short-lived Long Island Steamship Co., Reuben H. Wilson, president, to link the village with New York City. They were soon forced to default for lack of business.

84. HTR, III, 452.

85. Bayles in Munsell, 86.

86. Port Jefferson *Echo,* June 30, 1927, 4.

87. Administrator's papers. Nehemiah Hand. March 12, 1895. SCSC. File 13041.

CHAPTER THREE

The Wealth of the Shipbuilders

The major occupation of the shipbuilders was, of course, shipbuilding and ship-repairing. It was through these industries that they made or lost the bulk of their wealth. The amount of an individual shipbuilder's wealth is difficult to gauge precisely. The best sources for financial information, bank accounts and other monetary records, have not survived— but two major sources of financial information are available. These are the incomplete declarations reported to the United States Censuses, which reveal only what the respondents wanted to tell, and the R.G. Dun and Company evaluations. The latter, conducted by professional agents, are presumably more reliable, since it was R.G. Dun and Company's business to make accurate assessments of assets available to potential creditors. Property-tax assessments and probate records can occasionally be found as well.

The following two tables from the United States Population Censuses (Table 3-1, page 60) and the records of R.G. Dun and Company (Table 3-2, page 61) estimate the wealth of major Suffolk County shipbuilders. The discrepancies indicate the danger of taking census figures as anything but the most general indicators. Unfortunately, the 1880 census did not include reports of real and personal wealth and the 1890 census was destroyed by fire. Table 3-2 contains a wider sampling of the yearly evaluations conducted by R.G. Dun and Company. These provide a more detailed picture of the financial situation of the shipbuilders throughout the larger part of their careers. Since R.G. Dun and Company assessments were not always chronologically synchronized, Table 3-2's yearly reports were selected to provide as much uniformity as possible. In all cases first and last reports are cited.

Where approximate chronological comparisons can be made it seems that the greatest discrepancies between the two tables occur in the 1870s. Here, the R.G. Dun and Company accounts show most shipbuilders increasing their wealth significantly while the Census reports depict them as either holding fast or only moderately improving. It should be noted that both Census and R.G. Dun and Company reports generally include wealth from all sources.

The status/wealth of the shipbuilders relative to their neighbors may be obtained through an analysis of census records. The real-estate section is omitted since it can become highly biased due to the high acreage possessed by some farmers. While personal estate was a vague designation covering a myriad of items from bedpans to gold coins, it would have included everything that represented liquid or near-liquid wealth. Since the population was supposed to be reporting on the same items, a comparison based on the personal-wealth section provides a general indication of the position of the shipbuilders relative to that of others in their communities. The Brookhaven returns for 1870 have been chosen for this analysis. Returns have been divided into seven monetary categories. The number of respondents per category and percentage of the total is given.

$0-200	$201-500	$501-800	$801-1000	$1001-3000	$3001-5000	over $5000
150	281	99	73	160	24	57
18%	33%	12%	9%	19%	3%	7%

Source: US Census of Population, Brookhaven Town, 1870

Personal Property Holdings in the Town of Brookhaven, 1870

The major Brookhaven Town shipbuilders fall into the top category of personal estate. James M. Bayles, John R. Mather, and J.J. Harris all possessed reported personal estates ranking them among the town's wealthiest citizens. Nehemiah Hand's listing was included with John E. Roe and amounted to $52,000 in personal estate. This business coupling seemed to indicate a partnership in a general store and paper manufactory.

R.G. Dun and Company records provide much more information regarding the shipbuilders than mere numbers. The firm's agents frequently commented on the builder's business practices, position in society, promptness of payments, financial difficulties and, occasionally, personal characteristics. Sometimes their estimation of a person's wealth was rendered in a descriptive phrase rather than a number. More infrequently, agents disagreed with each other about an evaluee. By their own admission, R.G. Dun and Company agents sometimes had difficulty approximating the financial status of the shipbuilders. This may partially account for some of the jumps or declines in builders' reported assets.

Commentary by R.G. Dun and Company investigators nevertheless provides a useful contemporary glimpse into the world of the nineteenth-century shipbuilders on a level at least formally superior to neighborhood gossip or myth. Not surprisingly, R.G. Dun and Company agents were most consistently impressed by the major builders: James M. and James E. Bayles, John R. Mather, Nehemiah Hand and Jesse Carll.

The most extensive chronological account of any Suffolk County shipbuilder's career in R.G. Dun and Company records is that of James M. Bayles. The first mention of Bayles occurs in an August 17, 1850, report concerning his joint enterprise with "Davis" in a store. This was probably some form of the general merchandise/chandlery which Bayles had inherited from his father.

Bayles was already worth $1500 and his and Davis' joint real estate holdings were given as $2000. When this enterprise was dissolved in 1853, Bayles was "considered abundantly safe" by the Dun and Company agent.[1] This confidence referred to his ability to repay credit. In December of that year Bayles' business activities were described as "large" in the shipyard and a "good deal" in the store. His total wealth was listed at $7000.[2] In the late 1850s and early 1860s Bayles is described as "doing well and...worthy of credit," "safe," abundantly responsible." By June 24, 1864, he was reported "worth altogether $15,000. Honest, industrious and worthy of credit."[3] By 1866 Bayles' sons, especially James E. who later took over the shipyard, began to appear in the reports. However, the "son [James E.] has no means outside his interest in the shipyard."[4]

During the late 1860s, positive evaluations of James M. Bayles compounded, and the early 1870s saw no halt in his increasing prosperity. The December 5, 1868, report reads "Doing very prosperous business and making money rapidly. Prompt good business man and perfectly reliable."[5] "Good for all they want," "all right in every respect," "Good firm well off and good pay, Enjoying good business," are other comments from this period.[6] The only break in this pattern occurred in 1878 when the October 12 report stated "not doing so well as formerly but are good for contracts, little slow at times, former est[imate] too high. Now est worth 25-30m/$."[7] This downturn in the late 1870s also shows up in the Dun records regarding Jesse Carll. Such declines probably reflect the lingering effects of the 1873 depression on the Island's builders. This is the sole Bayles report that notes any financial contraction or decline.

By 1881 the Bayleses were again "in first class standing and credit locally."[8] The R.G. Dun and Company report of February, 1883, stated that "$40-50m/$ is thought a fair estimate of means. Thought safe for all they will buy."[9] The December 13, 1883, evaluation identified James M. as "the monied man of the concern worth about $30-35m/$" while James E. was believed to possess $10-15,000. "Both are said to own real estate and are thought a safe risk for all their wants."[10] The last mention of the Bayleses in R.G. Dun records, 1888, comments that "the senior member of the firm does not give much attention to the bus[iness]. The son manages chiefly. Both are men of good business ability and have acquired considerable property. The son owns a house and a lot say [$4500] and the old gent owns a house and a lot say [$2500] besides both own considerable vessel property and the shipyard and railways. Their combined estates being say [$20-25,000]."[11] The most arresting thing about this last report is the drop of $20,000 in the estimated value of the father and son's assets. Some of this may have simply resulted from an overestimation in the 1883 report. It may also be partly attributable to the very real decline in shipbuilding in the late 1880s. It is also instructive to see that the R.G. Dun and Company agents were about a dozen years behind in reporting James M.'s

	1850		1860		1870	
	Personal	Real	Personal	Real	Personal	Real
Greenport						
Bishop, Oliver					$ 4,000	$6,000
Bishop, Hiram				$5,000		$1,200
Port Jefferson						
Bayles, James M.	$5,000	$8,000	$5,000	$8,000	$500	$8,000
Mather, John R.			$1,500	$3,000	$10,000	$10,000
Setauket						
Hand, Nehemiah			$1,500	$ 3,000	$1,000	
1870-Hand, George						
Northport						
Carll, Jesse					$20,000	$12,000
Jarvis, Jesse			$200	$3,000	$2,000	$15,000
Hartt, Samuel P.			$3,000	$10,000		$20,000
1870-Hartt, Erastus						

Source: U.S. Population Census, 1850,1860,1870.

TABLE 3-1

Estimated Wealth of Major Suffolk Shipbuilders Reported in U.S. Census

retirement and James E.'s succession to the position of "Boss" shipbuilder at the Bayles yard.

The first three entries for John R. Mather in the R.G. Dun and Company records do not include any financial estimates at all. The June 28, 1874, notice states that Mather was "Good for any amount he calls for. Worth a good deal of money."[12] Although the Bayleses outproduced Mather and were credited with greater financial assets, Mather was the more impressive individual to the R.G. Dun and Company reporters. The August, 1876, entry claims he was "probably the best man in town. Most capable."[13]

This view was expanded slightly on December 1, 1878, when the investigating agent described him as "an old settler, owned real estate and vessel ppty, stands well and seems easy financially. Very careful, one of our best men and is perfectly safe for all contracts."[14] Again, in December of 1881, "He has the name of being the best man in town, owns R[eal] E[state] [and] is doing a good bus. and is estimated 30,000-40,000. [He] is of good char[acter] and habits and good pay locally."[15] Mather's last R.G. Dun and Company report, from December, 1891, falls under his lumber partnership with his half-brother, William M. Jones. The lumber concern was "doing a prosperous bus[iness] and prompt pay in high credit."[16] The partnership's estimated worth was $60-70,000. Presumably at least half of it was Mather's. Whether this figure includes anything from his shipbuilding, which had fallen off by then, is undetermined.

	12/1853	6/1854	7/1870	12/1878	12/1881	2/1883	1/1885	9/1895	4/1898
Bayles, James M.	7,000	15,000	25,000	25-30,000	35-45,000	40-50,000	60,000	39,000	20-25,000
						12/1883		9/1895	
Bayles, James E.						10-15,000		15,000	
			5/1877	12/1881	12/1883			2/1888	12/1888
Mather, John R.				40,000	30-40,000	40,000		30,000	30-35,00
		7/1870	9/1874		9/1876				
Hand, Nehemiah		18-30,000			25-30,000	30-40,000			
						12/1878	1/1882	1/1885	
Hand, George						5-10,000	8-10,000	8-10,000	
	8/1868	2/1869	12/1873	4/1898		1/1882	10/1883		
Carll, Jesse	10,000	50,000	30,000	30,000		40,000	40,000		
	5/1867	2/1872	9/1874	4/1877					
Jarvis, Jesse	5,000	4,500	5,000	3,500					
	5/1867								
Hartt, Samuel P.	10-15,000								
			9/1874	9/1875					
Hartt, Erastus			2,000	2,500					

Source: R.G. Dun and Company

Table 3-2

Estimated Wealth of the Major Shipbuilders from the
Records of R. G. Dun and Company

If the R.G. Dun and Company agents liked Mather, they practically waxed rhapsodic over Nehemiah Hand. It seems they were much taken by his business acumen, and the picture that emerges from these necessarily terse entries strongly complements the picture that Hand painted of himself in his 1883 autobiographical account. The first mention of Hand, on July 26, 1870, is conventional. He was considered to be worth $18-30,000, allowing a considerable margin for error. He was described as a "good bus[iness] man doing well, considered safe for contracts."[17] However, the July 3, 1872, report gives a better indication of Hand's effect on R.G. Dun and Company evaluators. "He is a smart, shrewd and active businessman. Indus[trious] tem[perate] and prudent and he is undoubtedly good for $20,000. He builds large vessels by contract."[18] In 1874, Hand and his son, George, were described as of "good bus[iness] capac[ity] mkg money all right."[19] In 1876, they were "considered gd. for any amount they will buy."[20] The agent responsible for the 1877 report stated that "these men are real bus. men and own a large amount of property. Very good pay. Wealthy."[21]

Nehemiah Hand retired in 1878 and George Hand took over the business. R.G. Dun and Company agents continued to give the high praise they had given his father. On February 26, 1878, George was judged a "smart and gd. mechanic in good standing. Can't est[imate] the full amt of property of such people but [know] they pay for all they buy."[22] On January 25, 1881, R.G. Dun and Company reporters estimated George's real estate at $5000 and his personal wealth "as much or more without indebtedness." George, this evaluation went on, was a "smart and prosperous fellow and good pay. Pockets full of money always."[23] George's pockets might have been full of money, but the reports reveal that he was believed worth only half what his father had been. In an entry for the following August, George was deemed a "first class builder. Well to do in the world. Remarkably so for a young man."[24] George's last appearance in the R.G. Dun and Company accounts, January, 1885, is noticeably more subdued. He "does a nice safe bus."[25] His real estate was listed at $800 and his total wealth estimated as $10,000. The moderation of the description of George Hand's business runs parallel with its decline. George Hand abandoned shipbuilding in 1893 and took a job with the federal government. In the end the R.G. Dun and Company agents underestimated Nehemiah Hand's wealth. When he died in 1894, he left cash inheritances to his wife, children and grandchildren totaling $52,635. This sum, significantly higher than either census or R.G. Dun and Company estimates, indicates both frugality and investment. The figure was probably not the entire extent of his wealth.[26]

Jesse Carll was not only Northport's largest shipbuilder, but a man of considerable talent and significant financial connections—as his relationship with the New York City firm of Woodhouse and Rudd attests. The picture that materializes from the R.G. Dun and Company records is that of a capable, if undramatic, businessman. The first mention of Carll, August 27, 1865, reports the dissolution of his partnership with his brother, David. It goes on to describe him as "perfectly good. Good reputation etc."[27] By 1868 he was listed as the "largest shipbuilder here," and worth $10,000 excluding real estate.[28] An 1869 estimate of Jesse Carll's wealth at $50,000 is clearly an overevaluation, but throughout the 1869-1872 period he is described as "wealthy," and "wealthy A-1."[29] In 1873, the $50,000 figure reappears, but subsequent reckonings, probably more accurate, estimate his worth at $30,000 in 1875 and 1877.[30] James M. Bayles' setback in 1878 was anticipated by Carll's losses of the preceding year. The November 2, 1877 report states that Carll "has lost largely in vessel property during [the] past year but is still A-1 tho not so wealthy as formerly." Carll's wealth stood at its $30,000 estimate, however, and was revised upward to a possible $40,000 in September of 1878.[31] The last mention of Carll, October 10, 1883, reported he was "said to own RE clear. Doing good bus. and $40,000 is thought a safe estimate of his means. He is spoken of as being of good char[acter] that is good [pay?] locally and thought safe to credit."[32]

As in the case of Hand, either R.G. Dun and Company and the census grossly undervalued Carll's holdings or his fortune increased considerably from the time of the last available R.G. Dun and Company estimate until his death. His will, dated June 7, 1902, does not provide an itemized listing of his total assets. It does, however, list cash bequests amounting to $113,300.[33] Upon his death, the value of Carll's full estate, including property, was estimated at $250,000 in local newspapers.[34]

Of course, not all shipbuilders were as financially well off as Bayles, Mather, Hand or Carll. Nor were all considered as scrupulous. While not in the same league as the major shipbuilders, Jesse Jarvis of Northport had a long and active career in the industry. The glimpses provided by the Dun agents reveal a more precariously balanced business career which may have been a cause of what seems to have been questionable business practices. R.G. Dun and Company's first report on Jarvis, March 20, 1867, credited him with assets worth $5000 and "gd. for most bills. Slow pay but good."[35] However, the August 10, 1868, report described him as "tricky and not to be trusted."[36] The agent who wrote the April 9, 1869, report suggested that Jarvis might be having financial diffi-culties as his real estate was mortgaged. Nevertheless, the agent went on to say "I have never believed him to be tricky in his dealing. He has a large family."[37] Whether the last sentence was meant as evidence of probity or irresponsibility is unclear. Still, suggestions of financial problems continue. By November, 1869, R.G. Dun and Company investigators heard that his property was in his wife's name, a standard method for keeping it out of creditors' hands. The estimates of his real-estate assets held steady at $5000.[38]

The reports from 1870 to 1872 suggest that Jesse Jarvis regained some level of stability in his business. The February, 1872, entry credits him with a house and lot valued at $2000 in addition to his shipyard, which was reckoned at $2500. Jarvis employed five or six men at the time and was rated A-1.[39] But in 1873, a depression year, negative remarks begin to creep back into the reports. Although considered a "gd. clever man" about sixty, he was also deemed "a slow pay does but little...Cr[edit] should be small. He is not very desirable."[40] Again in February, 1874, Dun agents stated he "didn't do much bus. Sharp trader and industrious but is slow pay." In March, 1875, he was said to be "a little sharp in bus. matters."[41] The reporter apparently meant that Jarvis was a little sharper in his own interests than he ought to be.

Perhaps this unethical behavior, if it was that, was an attempt to stave off disaster. This was the same period when major builders such as Carll and Bayles also had setbacks. Jarvis, a more marginal, undercapitalized, businessman, would have been more seriously affected and might not survive. In October, 1875, Jarvis' property was described as heavily mortgaged and he himself was called a "poor pay."[42] In April, 1877, R.G. Dun and Company reported him out of business. Either this report was premature or somehow Jarvis managed to reestablish himself, since he reappears in the R.G. Dun and Company records for 1882 and 1883. These entries clearly describe a man going under. The January 19, 1882, account relates that Jarvis "has been sued several times and has held up some judgements." Surprisingly, the agent went on to report that "a claim for a moderate amount is probably collectable."[43] R.G. Dun and Company's last entry for Jarvis reports the collapse of his business. The February 10, 1883, entry explains he "has sold his shipyard to be delivered early in the Spring."[44]

However, this sale was not quite the end of Jesse Jarvis' career. Despite the loss of his shipyard, Jarvis still picked up an occasional contract. He repaired a steam yacht in May of 1885, and did some repairs as late as 1888. That same year he even built a small sloop. These latter jobs were done at space Jarvis rented at the Sammis commercial dock.[45] Now an old man, Jarvis gave up the fight and retired completely. He died ten years later. His tombstone in the Northport Rural Cemetery bears a relief carving of a ship's half model, symbolic of the trade he struggled so long and hard to practice.

Derivative Economic Activities

Shipbuilding generated considerable ancillary business activity. Sailmaking proved one of the larger and more enduring subsidiary maritime industries that carried over to the yachting days of the present century. Reuben H. Wilson of Port Jefferson established what became the largest sail loft in Suffolk County. Wilson, who may have been brought to Port Jefferson by James M. Bayles, began his operation in 1837 at the foot of Jones Street. His loft received the bulk of Port Jefferson's business and probably much else besides. He frequently experimented with new sail designs, and his "bird's wing" pattern has been credited by some local authorities as the first significant improvement in sail design in 2500 years.[46] It was Wilson who outfitted the yacht *America* when she won the "America's Cup" in England in the summer of 1851. As Wilson's business increased, so did his need for larger quarters. In the 1850s he moved to a block-long, three-story structure that stretched from the harbor to Water Street. After Reuben Wilson's death in 1876, his sons, Frederick M. and Advance, inherited the business. Advance eventually left for Boston where he established his own sail loft. Frederick M. was left to face the impact of the decline of shipbuilding, and the triumph of motor-driven vessels, on sailmaking.

Another important sailmaker was Nathan Fordham, who operated lofts at both Sag Harbor and Greenport during the 1870s. Northport had its own sail loft at the juncture of Main Street and Bayview Avenue, an enterprise started by Jesse Jarvis during the 1850s. By the 1880s it was owned and operated by William Mills after Jarvis fell on hard times.

In addition to Reuben Wilson's sail loft, Port Jefferson also boasted tinsmiths, shipsmiths and chandlers who were largely, if not exclusively, dependent upon local shipbuilders. Some craftsmen plied their specialized, artisanal, trade through private contract rather than working full-time under any particular builder. This was true of some of the ship riggers and ship joiners as well, and also the skilled woodcarvers who shaped the more elaborate interior joinerwork or did ornamental work such as nameboards and figureheads. George H. Buck was the main ornamental carver in Port Jefferson while John Bunce held the same position in Northport. The shipsmiths Ezra Hart and A.T. Sturtevant were proprietors of busy shops along the Port Jefferson waterfront and were reported to have owned "substantial homes." Obviously, these specially skilled craftsmen depended on the health of Long Island's shipbuilding industry for their livelihood.

The importance of shipbuilding to the villages on the northern shore of Suffolk was immense and was frequently commented upon by contemporary writers. In 1874, Northport was judged the most flourishing village in Huntington Town. The observer clearly believed that the three shipyards he saw in operation were a major contribution to Northport's prosperity.[47] Munsell's 1883 history of Suffolk credits James M. Bayles' workforce of 50 men as "largely contributing to the prosperity of the village."[48] Nor was this an isolated opinion. Upon Bayles' death in 1889, the Port Jefferson *Times* concluded, "While his shipbuilding enterprise may have been of great pecuniary advantage to himself, it also was of considerable benefit to Port Jefferson—more so than any other business enterprise here."[49]

Long Island shipbuilding enjoyed two boom periods when its importance to the local economy was greatest. The first occurred in 1845-55, when the largest number of vessels was recorded; the second during the 1870s, when the highest tonnage was launched. According to the decennial census figures, which are somewhat at odds with figures from other sources,[50] the Suffolk workforce increased enormously between 1850 and 1860. After that, there was a continual decline.

The ten-year census interval may preclude the possibility of quantifying the Suffolk workforce at its peak before the Civil War. All authorities agree that the

The Robert Mills sail loft at Glenwood Landing, circa 1875.

1845-58 period was the most expansive for shipbuilding nationally. By the time the 1860 census was taken the industry had already contracted and the impact of that heady period on Suffolk's villages was lost. Nehemiah Hand recalled that in 1855 "Setauket was a lively place...from 90 to 100 men being constantly employed. Mechanics came from all quarters, more than there were houses for."[51] If Setauket employed 90-110 men, Port Jefferson must have had at least half again as many at the time, with smaller yards in secondary villages contributing yet more workers. A projected total of 250 shipbuilding workers in Brookhaven Town in 1855 seems realistic. Yet, five years later, the 1860 Census records only 151. Clearly, the years of full-throttle ship construction were skipped by the Census Office's ten-year hiatus.

Some approximation of the impact of the shipbuilding industry on these Long Island towns may be had by ascertaining the percentage of shipworkers among the general population of the villages. In 1870 Port Jefferson's population stood at about 2000.[52] The male population would have been around 1000, and deducting 250 to cover boys, the infirm and those too rich to work, a laboring population of 750 may be surmised. The 1870 census reports that there were 74 Port Jefferson men in shipbuilding, approximately ten percent of the work force. Similarly, in 1882, Northport contained a population of 1500.[53] Cutting that number in half to exclude women and subtracting a further 260 to omit children and men too old or wealthy to work, a labor force of 490 can be projected. The 1880 Census lists forty-nine Huntington Town men working in shipbuilding. No builders seem to have been active in Huntington outside of Northport. Consequently, shipbuilding probably accounted for about ten percent of Northport's working population.

The principal occupation in these towns during the nineteenth century was farming. Others were fishermen and sailors, storekeepers, agricultural suppliers and middlemen. By the latter part of the century there were some new industries such as a rubber factory in Setauket, brickyards in Huntington, ceramics factories in Huntington, and some specialized types of agriculture such as truck farming and cranberry production.

One other method that can be used to attempt an assessment of the importance of the shipyards to their villages entails determining the cost/prices of the vessels built there. None of the builders left a full record of the costs of all their vessels. The most complete accounting was given by Nehemiah Hand. Since it is not always clear whether he meant price when he wrote cost, his figures probably represent the latter. Consequently, his enterprises may have brought in more money than is calculated here. Hand did not provide a price for every ship, but average prices per ton are able to be computed for each of the major types of vessels. Additionally, his output was divided into two time periods, 1850-1860 and 1861-1871. Using this admittedly general method, Nehemiah Hand's income was $223,803 for 1850-1860 and $252,464 for the 1861-1871 decade. The 41-percent increase in prices during the latter decade would have canceled the increase in income which the 1861-1871 period registered over 1850-1860.[54]

How this income would have affected the Setauket area is as problematical as determining precisely what Hand realized from his ships. While some of the costs incurred by the shipowners translated into income for chandlers, lumber dealers, etc., outside Long Island, most of the money generated by the construction and sale of these vessels flowed through the economy of the shipbuilding villages. Local chandleries, lumber and hardware dealers, carters and smiths, not to mention the workers, were the prime beneficiaries of activities in the ship-yards. Much of the profits realized by the builders were returned to the local economy through domestic purchases such as food, clothing, houses, property repairs and entertainment. Additionally, shipbuilders sometimes took a prominent lead in the establishment of banks, as the Bayleses did in Port Jefferson. At least one builder, Nehemiah Hand, acted as a local money-lender. While the exact amount of money the builders generated in their villages cannot be known, the cost/price of their ships provides a crude but not unuseful indication of the possibilities.

Such figures do not, of course, explain the full importance of these ship-yards to their host communities. They do not tell us what percentage of village personal income was attributable to the shipyards. Nor do they answer the larger question of what portion of the villages' prosperity was dependent on ship-building. In this regard the observations of contemporaries are the best guide. Significantly, every major contemporary source credited shipbuilding and its ancillary trades with creating such prosperity as existed in Long Island's ship-building villages from 1840 to 1880.

Notes:

1. R.G. Dun and Company Collection. New York, Vol. 581, p. 78. Baker Library. Harvard University Graduate School of Business Administration.

2. Ibid.

3. Ibid.

4. Ibid., New York, Vol. 583, p. 320.

5. Ibid.

6. Ibid.

7. Ibid.

8. Ibid. New York, Vol. 585, p. 78.

9. Ibid.

10. Ibid.

11. Ibid., p. 780.

12. Ibid., New York, Vol. 584, p. 392.

13. Ibid.

14. Ibid.

15. Ibid.

16. Ibid., p. 893.

17. Ibid., p. 396.

18. Ibid.

19. Ibid.

20. Ibid.

21. Ibid.

22. Ibid.

23. Ibid., New York, Vol. 585, p. 436.

24. Ibid.

25. Ibid.

26. Administration Papers. Nehemiah Hand. March 12, 1895. SCSC. File 13014.

27. R.G. Dun and Company, New York, Vol. 582, p. 581.

28. Ibid.

29. Ibid.

30. Ibid.

31. Ibid.

32. Ibid.

33. Will of Jesse Carll. June 7, 1892. Liber 41, pp. 488-498. SCSC.

34. *Long Islander,* October 31, 1902, 1.

35. R.G. Dun and Company, New York, Vol. 582, p. 23.

36. Ibid.

37. Ibid.

38. Ibid.

39. Ibid.

40. Ibid.

41. Ibid.

42. Ibid.

43. Ibid.

44. Ibid.

45. *Long Islander*, May 5, 1885 and January 7, 1888.

46. Welles and Prios, 20.

47. Richard M. Bayles, *Historical and Descriptive Sketches of Suffolk County* (Port Jefferson: 1874), 162.

48. Richard M. Bayles in Munsell, 62.

49. PJT, April, 1889. Bayles Scrapbook, FCC.

50. The 1880 United States Census lists 49 men engaged in Huntington Town ship-building. Munsell states a minimum of 75 working for Jesse Carll alone.

51. Bayles in Munsell, 85.

52. Welles and Prios, 13.

53. Guy E. Johnston (compiler), *Detailed History and Description of the Original Township of*

Huntington, 1653-1800. (Northport, 1926), 136.

54. Consumer Price Index, 1800-1900, HSUS, 210-211.

CHAPTER FOUR

The Political and Social World of the Shipbuilders

Considering their wealth and prominence, it is unsurprising that the shipbuilders took their part in politics and government. Politically, the shipbuilders were strongly Democratic. The tendency to support the Democrats might be traceable to the strong anti-Federalist tradition in Suffolk County. However, the Democratic Party's opposition to high tariffs would certainly have won the hearts of shipbuilders who believed that tariffs drove up the costs of their vessels.Loyalty to the Democratic Party waxed strongest in Port Jefferson, renamed in honor of our third President. For example, in 1883, John R. Mather was described as "an uncompromising and consistent Democrat, and although he has never held any political office he has always been recognized as foremost in the councils of his party."[1]

Strongly Democratic Mather might have been, but there exists no evidence that he played any role in Democratic politics other than advisory or participatory. Mather's main competition in Port Jefferson, the Bayles family of shipbuilders, were also Democrats. However, they played a more active role in politics. The Bayleses' Democratic affiliation dates at least to Elisha, founder of the Port Jefferson branch, who was a major figure in the movement to change the name of the village from Drowned Meadow to Port Jefferson in 1836. Elisha's son, James M. Bayles, was, like Mather, characterized as a "consistent Democrat of the Jackson school."[2] Bayles served as Brookhaven Town Assessor for three years, highway commissioner for a like term, and sole trustee for the school district, again for three years.[3] Reportedly, he refused to run for any higher office.[4]

The most politically active of the Bayleses, or indeed of any Suffolk shipbuilding clan, was James M.'s son, James Elbert Bayles. James E., "Eb" to his friends, began his political career in the 1870s and remained active in Democratic circles and affairs well into the twentieth century. In 1876, he made an unsuccessful bid for state assemblyman. Surviving correspondence indicates that he was already an inside member of the Democratic hierarchy in Suffolk County. Bayles' available political correspondence is both intriguing and frustrating since only letters written to him have survived. Consequently, some of the machinations and campaigns must be surmised from half the evidence. Nevertheless, what remains provides an intimate view of nineteenth-century politics as practiced on a local level.

Among James E. Bayles' correspondents was H.A. Reeves, perhaps the most influential Democratic leader in Suffolk after the Civil War. Reeves' power base owed much to his position as editor of the Greenport *Republican Watchman* which, despite its name, was a fiercely Democratic publication. Reeves often contacted Bayles to recommend persons deserving of favors, the nature of which

James Madison Bayles

is not always clear. Bayles was in contact with Democratic leaders throughout Suffolk and into Queens and New York City as well. On October 27, 1876, while he himself was running for state assemblyman, he received a note from A.W. Ketcham, a Democratic leader in Patchogue, requesting information on the amount due Suffolk Democrats from the state party war chest. Ketcham, finance chairman of "our Democratic Club... found we have to resort to every honorable way to raise sufficient funds to conduct this campaign which is quite warm with us just now. Many of our Democratic citizens have responded by way of subscription very liberally and many of them think the funds due this district should be applied in such a way that it will help our club out financially."[5] In the same year, the sailmaker Reuben H. Wilson of Port Jefferson had been an ardent promoter of Governor Samuel J. Tilden's campaign in the eastern part of the state. He did not live to see the "shameful" inauguration of Rutherford B. Hayes the following year.

If the state Democrats redistributed sufficient funds for their Suffolk candidates it did not help Bayles, who went down to defeat. Undaunted, the shipbuilder-cum-politician remained an active organizer and maintained an intense political correspondence. Although Bayles was unable to gain the assembly seat, the Democratic candidate for the Congressional district that encompassed Queens and Suffolk, James W. Covert of Flushing, New York, was returned to the Forty-fifth Congress.

James Elbert Bayles

Despite his loss, Bayles' standing in the party was solid enough for him to press for a political post for his friend, Frederick M. Wilson, the sailmaker, and his brother and partner in the ship chandlery, G. Frank Bayles. On December 24, 1877, Covert replied to a missive from Bayles with a note indicative of Bayles' political position:

"Application has been made to the War Department in the matter of your friend Mr. Wilson—but up to the time of my leaving Washington no response had been made.

"Will push the matter and do all I can for your friend. May I so far trespass upon your time and kindness to ask that you may forward to me a list of names of Democrats and a few Conservatives in your place, to whom I could send an occasional public document. This would place me under a great obligation."[6]

Covert was unsuccessful in gaining a government place for Frederick Wilson at that time. About 20 years later, in 1897 under Grover Cleveland's administration, Wilson was appointed Deputy Internal Revenue Collector for the Third Division of the First District. Bayles' role, if any, in this appointment is not known. It is instructive that Port Jefferson's leading sailmaker was also a Democrat.

Although James E. Bayles proved unsuccessful in finding a government post for Wilson, he pressed Covert to have his brother, G. Frank Bayles, named Supervisor of the Port Jefferson Custom House. On May 13, 1878, Covert sent a short note to Bayles telling him "your brother's appointment was confirmed by the Senate today."[7]

During the congressional race of 1878, Bayles again played the role of a party leader and organizer. On November 1, 1878, the Democratic candidate for county coroner, E. Forest Preston of Amityville, wrote Bayles asking him to distribute what was apparently campaign literature "quietly among our Republican friends who might wish to vote for me if they could do so easily." Preston then offered his analysis of the campaign to date. "I believe this town will support the ticket completely so far as the County goes, but have reason to fear that Covert will run very much behind in this region. For me, I shall do all I can to help elect him, but it drags heavily; there is considerable chagrin at the treatment Suffolk received at Jamaica, and the people don't seem to swallow it."[8]

Preston's message may have caused Bayles special anxiety since something had snagged his brother's appointment to the custom-house post. However, regardless of whatever slight some Suffolk Democrats thought they had suffered at the Jamaica caucus, Covert was returned again. Although Bayles' end of the correspondence has not survived, it seems he immediately contacted the congressman regarding his brother's posting. On November 11, 1878, about a week after the elections, Covert responded to Bayles:

"I don't suppose any change can be made in your brother's position till

Congress meets. Meanwhile, however, I have taken the precaution to write on to Washington, to friends there, asking them to put out every effort to keep him in...if necessary [I] will go at once to Washington to see Secty Sherman."[9]

Covert then went on to thank Bayles for his aid in the Congressional campaign. The terms used are highly revealing of the esteem in which Bayles was held by other Democrats. "The result," Covert continued, "was glorious and Suffolk did nobly. It is useless for me to attempt to thank you in mere words for all your kindness. Believe me I feel more deeply than I can express, all you have done for me."[10] Shortly after, G. Frank Bayles received his appointment as Supervisor of the Customs and Port of Port Jefferson.

Throughout the remainder of the 1870s and into the 1880s, James Bayles was the recipient of more requests for aid from those running for office. He also continued to work closely with H.A. Reeves of Greenport in intra-party affairs. The presidential election year of 1880 saw Bayles and Reeves hard at work trying to secure every possible advantage for Democratic candidates. A letter from Reeves to Bayles on October 12, 1880, illustrates some of their tactics:

"We must do all we can to get the vote for [Winfield Scott] Hancock [Presidential candidate] at any rate...two things need early attention. Absentee voters, how many can be got to come home and vote, and what the probable expense of doing so if we pay all or part of their expenses...Also in some districts, how many can be naturalized, that is, take out their final papers and what would it cost to send them to New York or Brooklyn [to complete the naturalization process].".[11] Whatever their success in getting out the absentee vote and naturalizing prospective voters, Bayles and Reeves saw Hancock go down to defeat before the Republican James A. Garfield of Ohio.

Interestingly, despite the political leverage he had amassed, Bayles never sought appointive office for himself. Apparently, he preferred to remain in Port Jefferson functioning as a local power broker. It was not until 1884 that he ran for office again, contending for the post of Brookhaven Town Supervisor. This position allowed him to remain at home and would not interfere with his partisan political activities. Successful in this election, Bayles was reelected the following year. During this latter term he also served as president of the Brookhaven Board of Health.

The most enduring legacy of Bayles' tenure as Town Supervisor was the replacement of Town meetings with election districts for Town elections. By permitting the citizens to vote in their own locales rather than making what could be a long trek to the Town seat in order to vote, Bayles' action served the process of democratization.

Bayles was apparently a genial man with pleasant features and a short pointed mustache. He proved highly popular as Brookhaven's Supervisor. An 1884 New York *World* profile of the Suffolk County Board of Supervisors provides an interesting contemporary glimpse of Bayles while he was in office.

"The best looking man on the Board, so the ladies say, and every morning the gentleman from Brookhaven smilingly responds to roll call from behind a bright new buttonhole bouquet, imported for the occasion.

"He is quite a joker, but many of his jokes are quite too serious to be amusing. One of his latest was his nearly successful attempt to joke a Republican Board into affording special comfort and encouragement to a fierce Democratic partisan newspaper. He explained the matter only as a joke."[12]

Bayles never held public office after 1885. Yet surviving evidence indicates that he retained his interests and at least some of his influence. Generally, however, there seems to have been a falling off in his political activity after 1890.

No other shipbuilder came close to approaching James E. Bayles in political interests and activities. Nehemiah Hand served as Town Assessor during the Civil War years. Never comfortable with incurring debt on his own account, he carried the same attitude into his office. Hand was proud of the fact that Brookhaven raised $85,000 through taxes rather than bonding in order to give its soldiers a $300 bounty.[13] In 1893, Hand's son, George, was made Inspector of Hulls at the New York Custom House. No builders in Northport or Greenport held public office, although Jesse Carll was known to be a Democrat.

Shipbuilders were often members, and sometimes leaders, of organizations whose primary function was social or quasi-political. In addition to belonging to such professional organizations as the National Association of Engineers and Boat Builders, Navy League, American Geological Society and the Belle Terre Club, James E. Bayles was a prime mover in the creation of the Port Jefferson Volunteer Fire Department. He served as its first president. Frederick Wilson, who operated Port Jefferson's leading sail loft, devoted much of his time to founding the Law and Order League and later became an agent for the Society of the Prevention of Cruelty to Children. Wilson also served as president of the Cedar Hill Cemetery Association which provided the village with a place of interment on the then-fashionable garden cemetery model.

Hardly surprising considering Suffolk County's ethnic make-up, all the shipbuilders were Protestant. Some, however, were considerably more active religiously than others. David B. Bayles of Setauket was perhaps the most religiously oriented builder. He joined the Setauket Presbyterian Church in 1843 and served as an elder from 1854 until his death in 1892. He was also the first superintendent of the church's Sunday school. Bayles was reported to have contributed to churches other than his own. Jesse Jarvis, who once held a brief appointment as inspector of elections, was an original subscriber to the Union Meeting House in Centerport, which was shared by Methodist and Presbyterian congregations. In 1873, the R.G. Dun and Company agent remarked that Jarvis was a "strong spiritualist." Whether this counted for or against him was left unstated.[14] Nathaniel R. White, a lesser Northport builder, donated $2000 for the building of St. Paul's Methodist Episcopal Church in 1855.[15] The religious beliefs of the Bayleses were less precise. Baptist, Presbyterian and Methodist ministers all presided at James M. Bayles' funeral service on April 1, 1889. The presence of all three of the village's major religious leaders served as a testament to the builder's prominence in local society rather than any denominational adherence. Jesse Carll never officially joined any church but frequently attended St. Paul's Methodist Episcopal Church in Northport. Both he and James E. Bayles were Masons. At the time of his death in 1929, Bayles was the oldest Mason in Suffolk County.

In general, the shipbuilding community was not highly involved in the major reform movements of the time. James M. Bayles, however, was "an active advocate of temperance" and the wife of Erastus Hartt was president of the local chapter of the Women's Christian Temperance Union in 1895. The wives of the shipbuilders were often reported to be engaged in charitable and social activities. Mrs. Jesse Carll, for example, was a member of the St. Paul's Ladies Aid Society, while Mrs. James E. Bayles was engaged in the Port Jefferson Literary Society.

Wealthy and secure in their social positions, the shipbuilders constructed homes commensurate with their status. These were not the ornate, resplendent English manor houses built by the great "Gilded Age" entrepreneurs on the North Shore Gold Coast or at Newport. Rather they were large attractive structures that followed Victorian architectural patterns. The homes of both Bayleses, Jesse Carll and Samuel Prior Hartt looked out over their respective harbors and shipyards. In fact, James M., James E. and G.F. Bayles resided on "Cookie Hill," from which slopes they could view all the activities in the harbor from Main Street to the Sound. John R. Mather lived in a similar house on Prospect Street which provided no water view.

Nehemiah Hand's home on Bayview Avenue in East Setauket gave him a commanding view of his shipyard, although it lacked the vista of the Bayles compound. Hand, a man whose cantankerous nature may have been the result of an early bout of rheumatism which, in his words, "left me a cripple for life,"[16] was disliked by his neighbors. After the Civil War he entered a dispute with several of them regarding the proper name of the road which connected Main Street (North Country Road) with Shore Road on the harbor. Hand insisted it be called "Hand Avenue," while his neighbors were equally adamant that it be named Bayview Avenue. For some time before his death a war of signs took place with Hand erecting markers reading "Hand Avenue." These would be torn down and replaced with new signs lettered "Bayview Avenue." Hand would then remove these replacements, causing the battle to start all over again. After his father's death, George Hand gave up the struggle and the road became, uncontestedly, Bayview Avenue.

The builders and their families enjoyed the amenities their status offered. In 1883, John R. Mather, well-established in both shipbuilding and lumber, and increasingly able to rely on his son, John Titus Mather, in running his business, was profiled in the Port Jefferson *Times:*

"Socially he is a pleasant gentleman. He loves a good horse…and is frequently seen at the Gentleman's Driving Park holding the ribbons over his trotter. He has amassed a considerable fortune by his industry and is prepared to enjoy life comfortably in the midst of an interesting family and universally respected by his neighbors and acquaintances."[17]

Certainly the major shipbuilders knew how to throw a party. Among the most important occasions for villagers and their villages was the launching of a new vessel. Such festivities dated to colonial times, and the tradition continued through the nineteenth century. In June of 1841, Samuel P. Hartt invited his neighbors for refreshments at his house to celebrate the launching of a new

Jesse Carll's shipyard and home on Northport Harbor.

sloop.[18] As the industry grew, these celebrations, and the shipbuilder's role in them, expanded as well. In the spring of 1885, Jesse Carll began the construction of a new schooner for the New York Harbor Pilot Service. On May 1 of that year, five members of the New York Pilot's Association visited Northport to take a look at the vessel during construction. Suitably impressed, and claiming she would be the fastest to go out of New York Harbor, "they were highly entertained by Mr. Carll who in capacity of 'mine host' can not be beaten."[19]

The New York pilot schooner Jesse Carll, *built by the Jesse Carll shipyard and here depicted in one of Thomas Willis's ship portraits with silk sails in relief.*

Carll's hospitality toward the five pilots was only a portent of things to come. When the new little ship, named *Jesse Carll,* was launched the following August, Carll presided over a celebration of impressive proportions. Three hundred pilots, their friends and relatives were in attendance. The Reverend Mr. Thwing offered a short prayer and Carll's daughter, Maud, christened the ship. Then the party began:

"Many of the ladies and gentlemen were highly entertained at Mr. Carll's residence, where everything to quench the thirst and to satisfy the hunger could be found in abundance. A band of music from the City was in attendance and played many popular airs."[20]

It was a sign of how times had changed when John T. Mather refused requests for a celebration on the launching of the 218-foot schooner *Martha E. Wallace* in 1902. He feared someone might be hurt in the process. Nevertheless, some 2000 people watched the launching ceremony from the ferry dock on August 2, 1902, despite a heavy downpour.

Family celebrations were often equally festive and elaborate. When James E. Bayles and his first wife celebrated their tenth anniversary they held a masquerade party where local newsmen found "great pains and no little expense had been resorted to."

Perhaps the most opulent celebration undertaken by a shipbuilding family occurred in 1885 when Jesse Carll's daughter, Hanie, married Carll S. Burr, scion of a wealthy and influential Commack clan. Two hundred fifty guests were present, "and the ladies were attired in elegant silks and satins and the glitter of the jewels would dazzle the eye of one unaccustomed to such an elaborate scene."[21] Bernstein's band from the City, apparently one of the favored society orchestras, provided the music. Nor was that all. Floral decorations "were under the auspices of the celebrated Seagram of Brooklyn...The supper was under the management of Dexter of New York fame. The game pie, an immense pyramid and magnificent specimen of culinary art from Delmonico's, was a present from Mr. Joseph Rudd of New York to Messrs. Jesse Carll and Carll Burr."[22] The somewhat dazed *Long Islander* reporter then went on to chronicle the impressive and expensive list of wedding presents. It is instructive that the Carll party not only took its model from City practices but imported City professionals to manage the affair.

The launching parties, masques, opulent weddings and gentrified amusements took place in the golden light of what was to be the Suffolk shipbuilders' Indian Summer. Changes in technology and in international and national trade had already begun to undermine the industry that had made such activities possible. Fifteen years after Jesse Carll gave his daughter away amid jewels, silk gowns and New York City caterers, shipbuilding was a rapidly failing industry, its previous vitality becoming memory as it hurtled down the road to extinction.

Notes:

1. Port Jefferson *Times*, November 10, 1883, 3.
2. Richard M. Bayles, "Brookhaven" in *Munsell's History of Suffolk County* (New York: W.W. Munsell and Co., 1883), 62.
3. Ibid., 61.
4. Brooklyn *Times*, 1889, clipping, Bayles Scrapbook, Frank & Frances Child Collection.
5. A.W. Ketcham to James E. Bayles, 10/27/1876. Typescript. FFCC.
6. James W. Covert to JEB, 12/24/1877. Typescript, FFCC.
7. J.W. Covert to JEB, 5/13/1878. Typescript, FFCC.
8. E.F. Preston to JEB, 11/01/1878. Typescript, FFCC.
9. JWC to JEB, 11/11/1878. Typescript, FFCC.
10. Ibid.
11. H.A. Reeves to JEB, 10/12/1880. Typescript, FFCC.
12. New York *World*, 1884. Clipping, Bayles Scrapbook, FFCC.
13. Bayles in Munsell, 61.
14. Collection of R.G. Dun and Company, New York, 1, 23. Baker Library. Harvard Graduate School of Business Administration.
15. *Long Islander,* 02/27/1855.
16. Bayles in Munsell, 84.
17. PJT, 11/10/1883, 3.
18. *Long Islander,* 06/25/1841, 2.

19. Ibid., 5/5/1885, 3.
20. Ibid., 8/14, 1885.
21. *Long Islander,* 11/20/1885, 3.
22. Ibid.

Chapter Five

Labor

Like most pre-industrial-revolution industries, shipbuilding was primarily a handicraft business rather than the emerging factory type.[1] The techniques of construction were rudimentary and readily acquired through a few seasons' work with a master ship carpenter. Since little "start-up" capital was required, it was relatively easy for a master ship carpenter or would-be master to set up his own yard and exist on an order-to-order basis like most house builders. A ready supply of labor was available locally, especially from those who had some experience in house carpentry or joining. Even agricultural workers might be taught some shipbuilding skills in a brief period of time and thus supplement their farming incomes. In time the more adept of these might quit agriculture entirely. The early shipyards were managed by a working master carpenter or shipwright personally overseeing the men he had probably trained without formal apprenticeship. These workmen, as shall be demonstrated, were overwhelmingly local in origin. Nevertheless, some youths were formally indentured into shipbuilding or one of its attendant crafts.

Wages in shipbuilding increased slightly over the course of the century, although a conscious attempt to hold them down became noticeable after 1880. Generally, wages tended to be higher in urban areas, lower in rural, as the following figures indicate.

1840	$1.00-1.50	rural
	$1.75-2.00	urban
1850	$1.75-2.00	rural
	$2.00-4.00	urban

TABLE 5-1[2]
Wages Paid per Day in Shipbuilding, 1840-1850

The lower wages (and costs) in rural or peripheral regions were well-established in colonial times. A similar situation existed in England.[3] The spread between the highest and lowest wages no doubt reflects wage differentials between the various skill levels as well as among the regions and cities surveyed. It probably depended to some extent on the availability of alternative employment. Actual take-home pay at any time depended, of course, upon the level of business and the amount of work available.

The lowest level of shipyard worker was the apprentice. Some indication of

A work crew pauses for its portrait at the Bayles shipyard, 1884, during construction of the three-masted schooner Nettie Shipman.

the conditions among apprentices at the beginning of the period may be gained from the 1825 indenture drawn up between master carpenter Stephen Smith of New York and the parent of the youth, John Englis. Englis learned his craft so well that he went on to become one of the leading shipbuilders of Greenpoint, Brooklyn.

The indenture was a traditional, paternalistic document, essentially unchanged from the colonial period. Young Englis was promised to be loyal, moral ("dice or any unlawful game he shall not play...nor haunt ale houses or playhouses") and unmarried. The apprenticeship was to last four years two months and seven days, and Englis was to receive two dollars and fifty cents weekly, plus ten dollars every three months "in lieu of eat, drink, washing, lodging, clothing and all other necessities."[4] Surviving evidence indicates that the wages paid to Suffolk County shipyard workers corresponded roughly to the industry norm.

The $2.50 weekly wages given Englis as an apprentice may be compared with that allowed to Jesse Howell when he entered the trade in February of 1857 at Setauket. Young Howell was to receive seven shillings per day the first year, eight the second and nine the third.[5] The use of the British monetary reckoning, increasingly anachronistic by 1857, presents some difficulties in computing Howell's wages. From other entries it seems that shipyard owner David Bayles reckoned a shilling at about twelve and one-half cents. This would mean that the apprentice earned about eighty-seven and one-half cents per day—about $4.50 a week. While Howell's wages also compare favorably with the fifty to seventy-eight cents per day that apprentices made in City yards in the 1840s, they were low compared to shipworker wages listed in table 5-1. However, Howell was only an apprentice and 1857 was a depression year.[6] Other figures suggest that Suffolk County wages kept pace with regional norms. This is supported by the fact that in 1854 Bayles paid his workers between twelve and seventeen shillings a day, which amounts to between $1.50 and $2.04.[7] This rate would put his wages within reach of although a little below the rural average of the decade. That this was standard pay in David Bayles' yard is borne out by his entry for wages given to George W. Hawken, whose $82.50 for 55 days' work comes out to $1.50 per day.[8] Such a wage policy seems standard for Suffolk County. Bayles' account book demonstrates that "country wages"—i.e., commodities—made up part of a shipyard worker's pay. Half bushels of turnips, sweet potatoes and potatoes supplemented the cash salaries Bayles gave his workers.

By 1865, at the height of the Civil War inflation, Nehemiah Hand was paying his men an average of $4.00 a day. Of course, money supply had increased and living costs had risen 64 percent between the two dates, and this diminished any real gains for the laborers.[9] It should be noted that more money could be made by those with more specialized skills. Craftsmen such as John Maloy, who did specialty painting, or John Bunce, who did Carll's decorative carving, certainly made above-average wages.

Working conditions moderated only slightly during the century. In 1800 the workday ran from sunrise to sunset. Between 1830 and 1880 the 10-hour day became predominant.[10] Following a custom established in colonial times, a ration of grog, usually served at 11:00 A.M. and 4:00 P.M., was part of the daily wages of the workers.[11] A Setauket account book from 1825 includes $14.12 for a barrel of rum among the costs of building a ship.[12] The grog-ration tradition appears to have died out by the time of the Civil War, perhaps an early victim of the temperance movement. It appears likely that pre-Civil-War labor relations were good, or at least personal, since master carpenters worked alongside their employees, who were frequently neighbors as well. Even later, when the business had matured and a more modern division of labor had emerged, there is little evidence to suggest labor-management problems that were not manageable on a face-to-face basis. In 1883, John R. Mather was described as "particular about every detail of his work. He lays out the timber himself, and carefully superintends its putting together. During the construction of a vessel he is daily at his post carefully directing the work."[13]

The only known exception to the generalization of peaceful labor relations was Nehemiah Hand. Toward the end of the Civil War, Hand was faced with a strike among his workers. As he later recalled the incident, "We were paying our men $4.00 for ten hours work. They struck for the same pay and eight hours work. We refused to pay and I went to Albany to buy timber for a house."[14] The apparent non-sequitur in the last sentence disguises a lockout, which Hand obviously won since he made no reference to capitulation and remained in business. Interestingly, Hand's strike occurred just one year before the great New York City shipworkers' strike of 1866. The City shipyard workers' wages had almost doubled during the Civil War, and the yard owners became concerned that their labor costs were pricing them out of the market. As a result, the owners stood their ground and the strike collapsed. Nevertheless, the strike sealed the doom of New York City as a shipbuilding center. During the strike work was sent "further east" and never returned. Indeed, Suffolk County shipbuilders probably benefitted from the collapse of the City shipyards. It may say something about Hand himself that he was the only local shipbuilder known to have faced a strike by his workers.

An approximation of the wealth of the shipyard workers may be achieved through an analysis of various sources. Evidence of average daily wages provides some indication, although it makes no allowance for wage differentials among various skill levels. Nor does it suggest anything about the possibility of savings for the acquisition of houses or other assets. A better understanding of the wealth of mid-nineteenth century shipyard workers may be gleaned from the Federal Manuscript censuses of 1860 and 1870. These returns provided for declarations of both real and personal assets. Personal estate was a vague term which might include furniture, bedding, jewelry or perhaps even livestock. Nevertheless, as it was likely to contain whatever liquid capital had been saved, or was available, it can be used as a very general indication of personal wealth. Unfortunately, there are few alternative sources of this type of information, and census information was voluntary and not all respondents obliged. The accuracy of such figures is generally non-verifiable. In addition, the 1880 census omitted questions on real and personal estate and the 1890 census was destroyed by fire. Consequently, it is impossible to pursue this method of inquiry into the late nineteenth century when the industry fell into its final decline. The Town of Brookhaven, which included the two shipbuilding centers of Port Jefferson and Setauket, and the boatbuilding village of Patchogue, is used for illustration in table 5-2.

Total Engaged in Shipbuilding: 151
Total Responding to Real-Estate Section: 72 (48%)
Low $50   High $4500
(all figures in current dollars)

Age	$50-500	$501-1000	over $1000
16-30	1	4	7
31-60	6	15	36
over 61			3

Total Responding to Personal-Estate Section: 39 (26%)
Low $100   High $8000

Age	$50-500	$501-1000	over $1000
16-30	4	2	1
31-60	14	3	11
over 61	1	1	2

Source: United States Population Census, Town of Brookhaven, 1860

TABLE 5-2

Wealth of Shipyard Workers, Town of Brookhaven, 1860

The respondents' estimation of their wealth is unusual, perhaps, in that it places so many in the higher categories. This accumulation is most dramatic in the real-estate section, where 64 percent reported holdings of $1000 or more. Even when the entire workforce is included—i.e., respondents and non-respondents combined—more than 30 percent of the ship workers reported assets of $1000 or over. This compares favorably with workingmen in Newburyport, Massachusetts, studied by Stephen Thernstrom. In 1860, only 11 percent of the Newburyport workers possessed real estate value in excess of $1000.[15] Possibly, some of the difference is ascribable to Newburyport's increasingly immigrant, largely Irish, population, people starting from nothing and unaccustomed to owning property. Nevertheless, Thernstrom's comment that "real estate was strikingly available to working-class men who remained in Newburyport for any length of time"[16] is applicable to Suffolk as well. The Newburyport and Brookhaven figures suggest that home ownership, at least outside the larger cities, was the norm rather than the exception among mid-nineteenth-century American workers.

Even the more elusive, and less thoroughly reported, personal-estate section shows 36 percent of the responding workers possessing assets of $1000 or more. Not surprisingly, men in the prime of their working careers had the greatest assets. The 31-60 age group, comprising 46 percent of all respondents, owned 78 percent of the real-estate assets valued over $1000, and 85 percent of all personal income in excess of $1000. The large number of high personal holdings suggests other sources of money or investments of prodigious frugality. The known parameters of shipbuilding wages indicate that such personal wealth

Percentage of Entire Workforce Reporting Real-Estate Assets		
$50-500	$501-1000	over $1000
5%	13%	30%

Percentage of Entire Workforce Reporting Personal-Estate Assets		
$50-500	$501-1000	over $1000
13%	4%	9%

Source: United States Population Census, Town of Brookhaven, 1860.

TABLE 5-2A

Percentage of Entire Workforce Reporting Real-Estate Assets

would be difficult to accumulate except over time or through inheritance.

The great unknown factor is the number who did not respond to either the real or personal-estate sections. The number of non-respondents—73—was large; it was 48 percent of the total number of workers. The age breakdown of non-respondents is illuminating.

It remains possible that some who reported no assets simply refused to cooperate with census officials for their private reasons—not least of which may have been suspicion of government officials and tax informants. It seems more likely that a majority of this group had negligible or no assets to report. This supposition is supported by the preponderance (53 percent) of non-reporters in the youngest age category, 16-30. Since this group would be dominated by

Age	
16-30	39
31-60	26
over 61	8

Source: United States Population Census, Town of Brookhaven, 1860.

TABLE 5-3

Non-Respondents to Real/Personal Estate, 1860

apprentices and those in the formative years of their careers, they would be least likely to have had the time or means to accumulate real or personal property. The next age group, comprising men in their peak earning years, 31-60, makes up 37 percent of the non-reporters. The situation was more serious for these men since the probability of their attaining real estate or other wealth, even at low levels, would most likely decrease or cease to exist as they aged further. If we assume that most of the 48 percent of workers who did not volunteer information had little or none to offer, the situation for a significant proportion of the industry's workforce was bleak indeed.

With a slightly smaller workforce and somewhat greater percentages of response, the general outline of workingmen's wealth in the Long Island ship-building towns exhibited some changes after 1860. Well over 50 percent of those responding still held real estate worth $1000 or more, and this is not far out of line with Thernstrom's Newburyport sample, where workers in that situation had increased to 42 percent of the city's laborers. However, the percentage of Long Island shipyard workers reporting personal property over $1000 declined to 15 percent in a decade, and those who held personal property between $50 and $500 rose from 48 percent in 1860 to 68 percent ten years later. The latter shift suggests some improvement among the lower echelons of the labor force and would reflect progress made by younger men as they moved into middle age. However, such an improvement would have been tempered by a 41 percent rise in consumer prices over the same decade, which might have rendered some of the gains in personal estate more apparent than real.[17] This moderate improvement is further indicated by the decline of non-respondents, those presumably without assets.

The non-respondents declined from nearly half the shipbuilding workforce in 1860 to one-quarter in 1870, again suggesting an improvement in the net wealth of workers. As should be expected, 56 percent of the non-respondents were under 30 and still in the early years of their careers. This amelioration of the financial condition of the workers may have resulted from the modest post-Civil-War boomlet felt in the peripheral shipbuilding regions after the collapse of the industry in New York City and other major urban areas. Nevertheless, it

Total Engaged in Shipbuilding: 127
Total Responding to Real-Estate Section: 88 (69%)
Low $150   High $6000
(All figures in current dollars)

Age	$50-500	$501-1000	over $1000
16-30	3	2	2
31-60	12	18	44
over 61	1	2	4

Total Responding to Personal-Property Section: 50 (39%)

Age	$450-500	$501-1000	over $1000
16-30	2	2	
31-60	24	9	6
over 61	5	11	2

TABLE 5-4
Wealth of Workers, Town of Brookhaven, 1870

was certainly an unhealthy sign that 25 percent of the workforce lacked real or personal wealth at the levels specified by the census-takers. This looks even more serious when it is combined with 18 percent owning less than $500 in real

Percentage of Entire Workforce Reporting Real-Estate Assets			
Value of Assets:	$50-500	$501-1000	over $1000
	13%	17%	33%

Percentage of Entire Workforce Reporting Personal Assets			
Value of Assets:	$50-500	$501-1000	over $1000
	24%	17%	6%

Source: United States Population Census, Town of Brookhaven, 1870

Table 5-4A
Percentage of Shipbuilding Workforce Reporting Assets

Age	
16-30	18
31-60	12
over 61	2

Source: United States Population Census, Town of Brookhaven, 1870

TABLE 5-5
Those Not Responding to Real/Personal Income, 1870

estate and 68 percent having no more than that amount in personal wealth. The substantial number of those with little and those with nothing is a further indication that, for the labor force, shipbuilding was not a lucrative profession. Worse, the gains of the boom that followed the Civil War were transitory. The succeeding decade would see wooden shipbuilding commence the decline from which there would be little or no reprieve.

Another method of appraising the financial status of the shipbuilding workforce is to gauge their real and personal holdings over a period of decades. Unfortunately, the federal censuses reveal only a small number who remained with the trade in any one village over 10 years. This small number may reflect the haphazard nature of the census techniques of the nineteenth century. Nevertheless, the result is a statistically weak sample. Excluding the builders themselves, ten men appear persistently in the Town of Brookhaven census records from 1860 to 1880. Again, the loss of the 1890 census makes itself felt. These men have been traced in the Town of Brookhaven tax records, with the results listed in Table 5-6, at right.

The Town's tax records demonstrate that, in terms of acquired assets, the workers were unable to advance themselves much between 1860 and 1880. The only jump in real property or personal income appears in the records of Adolphus Bayles. In 1900 his widow had tripled the previously reported personal holdings of 1880. Perhaps this improvement resulted from an insurance settlement. Indeed, it is uncertain if the Adolphus present in 1880 was the same man recorded earlier. Alan Bunce also seems to have tripled his personal assets, but had meanwhile reduced the size of his real-estate holdings. Again, it is not clear if this is the same Alan Bunce. Although the sample is small, the numbers support the observations of contemporaries, and the evidence of the census records, that shipbuilding work generally paid poorly throughout the century.

A salient feature of Suffolk County's shipbuilding workforce was its strong native character. In both Brookhaven and Huntington Towns the majority of names found in the records ran deep roots in the pre-1840 population. By way of demonstration, the following table (5-7) lists the total number of Brookhaven workers plus the number and origin of those not born in New York State:

Similarly, in Northport, of the 164 names of those engaged in shipbuilding between 1850 and 1880, only four were born in states other than New York. The foreign-born totaled a mere ten: two Englishmen, three Welshmen, two Irishers, a Scot, a Swede and a Prussian.[18] As was true in Brookhaven, the major-

	1860	1870	1880	1900
	Real-estate values are in acres with monetary values in parenthesis			
	RE PE	RE PE	RE PE	RE PE
Adams, J.J.	1/8 200	1/8 200	1/8 200	
Bayles, A.	1/4 300	1/4 100 (400)	10 400	10 1200
Bunce, A.	5 300	1/8 500 (200)	3/8 500	1/4 1500
Brown, G.	1/4 400	1/4 400	1/4 400	
Darling, C.	1/2 500	1/2 600	1/2 600	
Darling, L.	1/4 200	2 400	2 500	
Gildersleeve, E.			1/2 100	
Hart, E.	1/8 400	1/8 400	1/8 500	
Homan, B.	1/2 400	1/2 500	1/2 500	
West, E.	1/8 200		1/4 300	

Source: Brookhaven Town Tax Records

TABLE 5-6
Real and Personal Estate among Brookhaven Shipwrights

ity of the surnames of those working at shipbuilding in Huntington run deep in the town's history. Clearly, the Suffolk shipbuilders drew upon the local population for their labor, and it is equally evident that there was a reservoir of workers with requisite skills for the trade.

While the local character of the labor force remained constant throughout the century, it is not necessarily the same men who were continually employed in the industry. Census reports reveal a shifting labor force and fluctuating persistence rates. Although this may reflect flaws in the census reports and

	1850	1860	1870	1880
Total	47	151	127	92
Non-NY born	2	2	11	9

Origin of Non-NY Born:
1850: Massachusetts, England
1860: Delaware, England
1870: Maryland, Virginia, Connecticut, England 4,
     Scotland 2, Germany and Ireland
1880: Maine, Massachusetts, Connecticut, New Jersey,
     West Indies, Germany 2, England and Ireland

Source: United States Population Census: 1850, 1860, 1870, 1880

TABLE 5-7
Origin of Shipbuilding Workforce in the Town of Brookhaven:
State or Country of Birth

inevitable mortality, it most clearly underscores the volatile nature of the trade and the diminishing opportunities for young men in shipbuilding as the century wore on.

The persistence rates in shipbuilding in Huntington might actually have been somewhat better since six men listed in 1860 who are not reported as shipwrights in 1870 reappear as such in 1880. It is possible they quit shipbuilding temporarily and returned later. If they did, however, they are not listed in other occupations in 1870. Most likely they were simply missed in that census. If they are included in the 1870 persistence total they raise that number to 19, or 40 percent. If this is the case, the fall of the persistence rate in 1880 is dramatic.

There is little evidence of what became of shipworkers who fail to reappear on the censuses. Three men reported as shipwrights in 1860 appear in other occupations in 1870—one as a house carpenter, one a farm laborer and the last a carpet weaver. Only one man reported as a shipyard worker in 1870 is identified in a different trade in 1880. This was Richard Smith, a former sparmaker reported as a farmer. It must be presumed that the remainder of the men who disappeared from the shipbuilding trade had moved farther afield in search of their living.

The Brookhaven sample may be interpreted in several ways. The small

	1860	1870	1880
Number Employed	66	47	49

Present in 1860, remaining in 1870: 13 or 28%
Present in 1870, remaining in 1880: 13 or 27%

Source: United States Population Censuses: 1860, 1870, 1880.

TABLE 5-8
Persistence Rates of Shipwrights, Town of Huntington

number persevering in the trade from 1850 to 1860 may have been the result of the 1857 financial recession, which hit shipbuilding hard. Although the number who stayed with shipbuilding was generally consistent from 1860 to 1880, the figures reveal that about two-thirds of those employed by the Town's yards left and were replaced by others during that span. The turnover rates in both the Huntington and Brookhaven yards from 1870 to 1880 indicate that large numbers of men apparently found shipbuilding unremunerative, unpromising or unsatisfying and moved on. It should be added that there was a local tradition that farmers sometimes worked seasonally in the shipyards. The census figures

	1850	1860	1870	1880
Number Employed	47	151	127	92

Present in 1850, remaining in 1860:8 or 17%
Present in 1860, remaining in 1870: 43 or 38%
Present in 1870, remaining in 1880: 33 or 36%

Source: United States Manuscript Censuses, Town of Brookhaven, 1850-1880.

TABLE 5-9
Persistence Rates of Shipwrights, Town of Brookhaven

might be thrown off somewhat by respondents giving their principal occupation as the one they followed during a particular season. Nevertheless, the workforce showed more fluidity and volatility than might have been expected from one so profoundly local in nature. It seems likely that movement among workers primarily involved the least-skilled or those whose skills were less adaptable to other industries.

The migration of shipwrights during the nineteenth century was not an isolated phenomenon. Thernstrom reported that in Newburyport, Massachusetts, a city with a developing shoemaking industry "...less than half the unskilled labor listed in [Newburyport] on the censuses of 1850, 1860 and 1870 remained there for as long as a decade."[19] Apparently, Suffolk County shipwrights shared job/wage dissatisfaction and consequent migration with many other unskilled and semi-skilled American workers of the time.

The census of 1880, disappointing for its failure to inquire about real and personal estate, did take notice of those who were unemployed for one or more months during the preceding year. Twenty of Brookhaven's 92 shipyard workers (22%) reported some time unemployed.

The fact that one-fifth of the potential labor force was not fully employed suggests serious problems within the industry.

After the Civil War, wooden shipbuilding faced increasing pressure and competition from British-built vessels of iron and steel. The price of ships came to be determined in England, and wooden shipbuilders, whose products were less durable, had to offer their vessels at a lower price than a comparable ship built of metal.[20] With their costs of material rising, one of the few competitive measures remaining to the shipbuilders was reducing wages. For example, in 1850 wages paid to shipwrights vastly exceeded capital investment. By 1900, wages were less than one-third the average builder's total investment. The remainder was largely materials.[21] The state of Maine, which managed to main-

1-2	3-4	5-6	7-8
5	12	2	1

Source: United States Population Census, 1880.

TABLE 5-10
Months Reported Unemployed in Brookhaven Town, 1880

tain a significant wooden shipbuilding industry through World War I, did so primarily on the basis of lower labor costs, as the following comparison demonstrates.

There are some anomalies in these figures, which were volunteered by shipyard owners testifying before a House Committee investigating the decline of American navigation interests. The $3.50 high reported by one Maine builder is $1.50 higher than any other shipyard owner reported. Its accuracy seems questionable and it may skew the 1860 Maine figures upwardly. The Boston figure is very low for a large city, especially compared to New York where dissatisfied Boston workers could easily relocate. By 1870, excluding Navy yards, New York and Boston shipyards had been priced out of existence. The small gain in salaries in Maine, fifty-five cents a day, was eaten up by the 41-percent rise in the cost of living that occurred between 1860 and 1869.[22] Some of this rise was due to the difference between wage payments in specie before the war and

	New York	Boston	Maine
1854/60	$2.50	$1.50-2.00	low: $1.50 high:$3.50 average:$2.15
1869	$4.00	$3.00	low: $2.50 High:$3.00 average:$2.70

Source: Lynch Report

Table 5-11
Shipwrights' Wages Per Day

wages paid in currency after the conflict. Knowledgeable observers discounted currency by 30 percent.[23] The 41-percent decline in the purchasing value of money left the worker worse off in 1870 than he had been in 1860.

Ship production rose in cost from $55 a ton to $75 in the same period. Several Maine builders contended that the decline in the value of currency allowed ships to be built about as cheaply in 1869 as they were in 1860. On hearing this, the Chairman of the House Committee asked Cyrus F. Sargent, a Yarmouth, Maine, builder, whether "...instead of currency being a disadvantage, it is an advantage." The builder replied, "It operates against the laborer; it comes out of him."[24] Indeed, with the costs of metals and some woods exceeding any compensatory discount of currency, it is clear that Maine shipbuilders, and probably those elsewhere, relied on an effective decline in real wages to stay in the game at all.

These generally low prevailing wages account for the attraction federal shipyards held for shipbuilding workers. Several builders testifying before the Lynch Committee complained that their best men often deserted to the Navy yards. Not only did federal installations pay more, but they operated on an eight-hour day in contrast to the standard ten-hour day at privately-owned enterprises.

The falling wage factor certainly affected Suffolk County shipyards. Table 5-12 shows wages paid by the County's major builders. Precise statistical analysis is stymied by large omissions in the records of the United States Products of Industry. For instance, none of the Setauket/Port Jefferson shipbuilders were listed in the 1860 manufacturing census. The 1870 figures given for Jesse Carll are simply impossible—$60 per year or $1.25 a week. Some of the more glaring discrepancies in wages paid by individual shipbuilders may have resulted from faulty reporting by either the builder or the census-taker. It is most unlikely that Nehemiah Hand would have paid his workers so extravagantly in relation to his competitors. In his biographical account in *Munsell's History of Suffolk County*, Hand stated that he paid his men $4.00 in 1865. It seems doubtful he paid his workers more in less-inflated times. This certainly produces an inflated average wage for 1870.

Comparisons also rest on the assumption that wages in Northport in 1860 were roughly the same as those in Port Jefferson/Setauket. This seems most likely since the distance between the two centers was not great and the wages paid in Samuel Prior Hartt's yard in 1860 are in line with Brookhaven Town shipyard wages. With all this kept in mind the trend is visible. The great jump of 1854-60 reflects the boom of the "Golden Age," while the post-Civil-War decline indicates less advantageous times and the increasing pressure from iron and steel. The average wages in real dollars in Table 5-12, are based on a Bureau of Labor Statistics Consumer Price Index with a base year of 1967. Wage comparisons over such a long time span, even when deflated, are necessarily distorted due to enormous differences in the quantity, quality, or even existence, of goods and services. Nevertheless, the use of a standard dollar value demonstrates increases and decreases in wages independent of inflation, although the wage figures themselves are a purely theoretical device.[25] In 1880, Henry Hall reported wages ranging from $1.50 to $2.00 a day in Greenport and Port Jefferson and $1.50 to $2.50 in the South Shore boatbuilding villages,[26] confirming the chronic stagnation of shipwrights' wages.

The last glimpse of wooden shipwrights' wages comes from the 1900 Census of Manufacturers. In New York State, the average number of wooden-shipyard workers was reported as 3464 men who earned a total of $2,014,788, or $11.19 a week.[27] Since these figures are averaged from the entire state, it is difficult to determine if they completely mirror the Long Island situation, although it seems unlikely that Suffolk would have been far from the norm. However, $11.19 per week converts to $1.86 a day, which is less than the wages Hand and Carll paid 35 years previously. Fortunately for those still following the shipwright's trade, consumer prices were at approximately the same level in both periods and the decline was not worse in real dollars.[28] Nevertheless, the wages of men in wooden shipbuilding had remained stagnant and, more likely, had fallen in relation to the general working population. It should also be noted that the 1900 manufacturing census included in its shipwright category spar

Builder	1850		1860	1870
		(in current dollars)		
S. P. Hartt	$ 4.00		$10.00	incomplete figures
Jesse Jarvis			$10.00	
Jesse Carll			$10.00	
Darling and Darling			$ 3.12	
Mather and Hawkins			$ 3.75	
Bayles Bros.	$ 8.75			$ 7.90
N. Hand	$ 4.00			$14.00
S. Wines				$ 6.60
J. Harris				$11.00
E. M. Darling				$ 6.00
Average	$ 4.60		$10.00	$ 9.00
Average in real dollars (1967=100)	$18.40		$37.04	$23.68

Source: United States Census of Products of Industry , 1850, 1860, 1870.

TABLE 5-12
Weekly Wages Paid By Major Suffolk County Shipbuilders

and mast makers, boatbuilders and oar manufacturers. To what degree, if any, this skews the wage figure is impossible to determine.

In the 1880s, Long Island newspapers reported both the happiness new contracts induced among the general population of their towns and the increasing disillusionment of shipyard workers with the low wages offered.[29] The 1890-1914 period was one of continual decline. In this regard Welles and Prios are worth quoting at some length:

"One feature which had not noticeably changed in the average laborer's life...was the uniformly low wage. Local shipbuilders were paying bottom dollar for their labor. While papers trumpeted a surge of activity in the yards [the yacht building phase], reporting at least 16 steam yachts in various stages of construction in early 1899, local craftsmen were leaving in search of shorter working hours and higher pay. One contemporary newspaper account depicts shipcarpenters arriving in the village on the strength of an advertisement of job openings, only to turn away when the prevailing wage scale was revealed.[30"]

The disintegration of the Suffolk shipbuilding industry is reflected in the 1900 census. Brookhaven's shipbuilding force had fallen from 92 in 1880 to 63 in 1900. Two workers included in that count were located in Patchogue, indicating boatbuilding rather than genuine shipbuilding. While most laborers were still born in New York State, the census shows a dearth of local names, and this suggests that the County's residents no longer viewed shipbuilding as a viable occupation. Several Norwegians who were not noted previously were laboring in the diminished yards. There is also evidence of aging in the shipbuilding workforce. The average age of the shipwrights in 1850 was 35, in 1860 it was 29, in 1870 it was 39, and in 1880 it was 45. The average age of a shipyard worker in 1900 stood at 56.[31]

A sequence of the building of the schooner-yacht Palestine *is shown on the following pages. Here she is launched in 1904 by the Bayles yard.*

Stem and keel in place.

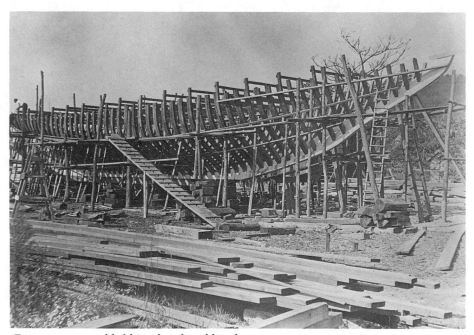

Frames set up and held in place by ribbands.

98

The interior of the vessel in progress.

Masts stepped and finishing details being put in.

Ready for launching.

The most striking indication of the decline of the industry lies in the unemployment figures. In 1880, 22 percent of the workers reported some time unemployed. In 1900, 48 percent had experienced at least one month's unemployment over the previous year. Twenty-two percent had six or more months without work. Eight men had not worked at all.[32] To be sure, the degree of hardship might not have been the same in all cases. George Hand, still describing himself as a shipbuilder, reported no work for 12 months. Actually, Hand had effectively folded up his operation in 1893, when he took a job as Inspector of Hulls at the New York Custom House. He certainly also benefited from some inheritance from his father. In his case such a report of unemployment is deceptive. We can guess that few, if any, of the other shipyard workers who reported unemployment were in Hand's position. There is no reason to doubt that the unemployment reported by the workers was anything other than painful—at least for those seeking work.

Interestingly, 41 of the shipyard workers owned their own homes, with only six reporting outstanding mortgages.[33] Three of the latter had experienced some unemployment and must have suffered the additional pressure of fear of the loss of their homes.

Small wonder that young boys were no longer training for the yards and shipyard workers were attracted to the last flourishing center of wooden shipbuilding. It is not known whether any Long Island shipwrights made the trek Down East. Whether they would have found Maine's prevailing wage satisfactory is doubtful. Consequently, many shipyard workers simply abandoned the craft altogether.

Notes:

1. Hutchins, John G.B., *The American Maritime Industries and Public Policy, 1789-1914* (Cambridge, Mass.: Harvard University Press, 1941), 79.

2. Ibid., 74.

3. Joseph A. Goldenberg, *Shipbuilding in Colonial America* (Charlottesville, Virginia, 1976), 95.

4. Cited in Fletcher, William L. *Historic Greenpoint* (Greenpoint Savings Bank, 1919), 32-33. Englis' $2.50 a week was better than the $1.50 Silas Hand made in Setauket that same year. Account Book 79-11, Mss. 3VPL.

5. D.B. Bayles Account Book, Mss. Three Village Public Library.

6. Morrison, John H. *History of New York Ship Yards* (Pt. Washington: Kennikat Press, 1970),95.

7. Bayles Account Book

8. Ibid.

9. United States Department of Commerce, Bureau of Labor Statistics. Consumer Price Index, 1800-1970. Series E 135-166. *Historical Statistics of the United States, Colonial Times to 1970* (Washington DC, 1975), 211.

10 . *Bi-Centennial History of Suffolk County,* 117.

11. Goldenberg, 96.

12 . Account Book 79-11, Mss. 3VPL.

13. Port Jefferson *Times,* November 10, 1883, 3.

14. Richard M. Bayles, "Brookhaven" in *Munsell's History of Suffolk County* (New York: W.W. Munsell and Co., 1882), 86.

15. Stephen Thernstrom, *Poverty and Progress, Social Mobility in a Nineteenth Century City* (New York: Antheneum, 1975), 119.

16. Ibid.

17. Consumer Price Index, 1800-1970, HSUS, 211.

18. Ibid., Town of Huntington.

19. Thernstrom, 96.

20. C.K. Hartley, "On the Persistence of Old Techniques. The Case of North American Wooden Shipbuilding." *Journal of Economic History,* XXXIII, No. 2, June, 1973, 374-375.

21. United States Department of Commerce, Bureau of Census, Twelfth Census of the United States, 1900. Volume X, Manufactures. Part IV, *Shipbuilding* by Alexander R. Smith, 213.

22. CPI, 1800-1970, HSUS, I, 210.

23. U.S. Congress, House. Report of the Select Committee on the Causes of the Reduction of American Tonnage. House of Representatives S, 28, 41st Congress, 2nd Session 1870. Hereafter cited as the Lynch Report, 143.

24. Ibid.

25. Computations were based on figures provided in CPI, 1880-1970, HSUS,I, 211.

26. United States Department of Commerce, Bureau of Census, United States Census of Population, 1880, Vol. VIII. *The Shipbuilding Industry of the United States,* by Henry Hall. (Washington, DC, 1884), 1991.

27. Smith, 229.

28. See BCH, 117 for Carll's wages and CPI, 1800-1970, HSUS, I, 211, for price levels in 1860 and 1900.

29. Welles and Prios, *Port Jefferson, Story of a Village,* 31.

30. Ibid., 41.

31. All figures from United States Census of Population, Town of Brookhaven, 1850, 1860, 1870, 1880, 1900.

32. All figures from United States Manuscript Census, Town of Brookhaven, 1900.

33. Ibid.

CHAPTER SIX

Decline

The end of the Civil War restored neither the full-blown shipbuilding nor the maritime prosperity that had existed before the conflict. In general, there was a continued decline in the American shipping industry and the yards which sustained it. Among American square-riggers, only Maine-built "Downeasters" maintained their competitive standing. This decline was felt most severely in the urban centers, where labor costs were high. The New York City industry, threatened with increasing labor and materials costs, suffered a disruptive strike and practically disappeared by 1870. To some degree the smaller yards in more peripheral areas, like those in Suffolk County, benefitted from the demise of the larger wooden shipbuilding enterprises since their cheaper labor and lower over-head allowed them to maintain their cost-competitiveness. Nevertheless, the pressures of policy, resources and technology were all running against the Long Island shipbuilders—as, indeed, they were running against American shipbuild-ing almost everywhere. The better-established Suffolk County yards remained solvent and profitable until the middle of the 1880s. After that, their decline was precipitate, reflecting the national competitive disadvantage.

The position of American shipbuilding deteriorated after 1885 for several reasons. One reason was that it attracted less capital than previously. The half-billion dollars invested in shipbuilding nationally in 1861 was already exceeded fivefold by railroad, industry and banking investments. Consequently, even before the Civil War, shipbuilding was moribund compared to the newly emerging industries and financial opportunities. As T.F. Rowland, builder of the *Monitor,* put it in 1869, investors during the Civil War began to place their cap-ital where there was "more gain and less risk."[1] Additionally, some of the capital made through shipping and shipbuilding was channelled into rival industries.[2] Foreign subsidized vessels made deep inroads in the American market, especially after foreign vessels were allowed to register on an equal footing with American-built ships. On December 25, 1869, the *Republican Watchman* complained that "ten tons of foreign built vessels entered New York Harbor for each ton of American built shipping."[3] This proved no temporary aberration. In 1900 American-built vessels accounted for only 9.3 percent of ships engaged in for-eign trade.[4]

The inexorable march of iron- and steel-hulled steamships also took an increasing toll of wooden shipping's former market. This was especially true in those overseas trades that required speed. The rise to dominance of the iron ship, and later the steel ship, decided Britain's reconquest of shipbuilding in both sail and steam. In the immediate post-Civil-War period, American maritime spokesmen were divided on the question of whether or not the United States could compete with British iron shipbuilders. More than a few believed that Britain's lead in the iron and steel industries gave them such a head start that American builders could not catch up—a conclusion in which modern researchers have concurred.[5]

Britain's comparative advantage in iron shipbuilding was partly based on a great price elasticity, since its iron production could be readily shifted from boilerplate to rails to shipbuilding metal. Consequently, according to C.K. Hartley, the price of British iron sailing ships fell from £17.4 a gross ton in 1856 to £10.9 a gross ton in 1890. The most dramatic decrease occurred in the 1880s owing to a fall in iron prices.[6] The rapid decline of American wooden shipbuilding in that decade can hardly be coincidental. Indeed, wooden shipbuilding may have persisted in places like Suffolk County and, more significantly, Maine, not because the builders were unaware of the new developments, but due to a lack of readily available alternatives and an immobile, or at least constant, labor supply. As mentioned previously, the only method American shipbuilders found for retaining some competitiveness with British iron vessels was to subtract the difference from labor.

In the international market, American builders of wooden and metal vessels were placed at a serious cost/price disadvantage due to heavy duties on foreign metal products, especially copper and iron. The regional shipbuilders never seem to have paid much attention to metal-hulled steam technology, and it remains doubtful whether they could have been competitive in the new shipbuilding even if they had. However, even in the construction of wooden vessels their costs were inflated owing to the expense of American copper and iron. A wooden vessel of 350 tons carried 75 tons in bolt and square iron, while copper was essential in sheathing hulls.[7] By 1869, tariff duties on copper and iron were 75 and 35 percent respectively.[8] According to some contemporary observers, the tariff raised the price of a 1000-ton ship eight to ten thousand dollars.[9] Not surprisingly, American shipbuilders recommended a "drawback" or subsidy to counteract the negative effects of the duties on copper, iron and sail cloth.[10]

The rise of American shipbuilding after 1800 had been greatly aided by the abundant, local, and readily exploitable supply of timber available to the builders. The low cost of this essential raw material went a long way toward providing American-built vessels a clear price advantage in the world market. Most of the easily harvestable and desirable timber was gone from East Coast shipbuilding regions before the Civil War. After 1865, most lumber had to travel great distances to the yards, with consequent fees from middlemen and shippers added to its price. While the price of iron plate in Britain fell from £10.10 a ton in 1856 to £5 a ton in 1888, wholesale lumber in the United States jumped from a Wood and Pearson Wholesale Price Index number of 52 in

1856 to 61 in 1886.[11] Shipbuilding lumber was also more expensive and specialized than housebuilding material, and relatively few species of trees were valuable to the trade and many of these were heavy. The specially shaped "natural-growth" white oak required for the curvature of the bow and most other frame members of a wooden ship were more costly yet. A process of bending shipbuilding lumber by steam to form the curved sections was available by 1855, but it never proved a complete economic success.[12] As a consequence of the dwindling of cheap and easily acquired materials, the competitive edge American shipbuilders had enjoyed was eroded or lost altogether by the 1870s.

To a limited degree the coasting trade made up some of the loss resulting from the decline of American vessels in international shipping after the Civil War. In 1863, 2,960,633 gross tons of shipping were moving cargoes on the coasts and tidal waterways of the United States. This number grew to 6,815,363 gross tons by 1914.[13] Of course, not all the coasting vessels were wood, although traditional ships' styles, especially schooners, predominated into the twentieth century and wood remained the material of choice. While the Suffolk builders derived some benefit from the expansion of coasting, Maine proved the big winner in ship orders. Although even Maine had depleted most

The coal schooner Emma M. Fox, *built in 1867 at Greenport by Hiram Bishop, and shown here delivering coal at Medford, Massachusetts.*

of its coastal timber, quantities could be floated down from the heavily forested interior, especially after the introduction of portable power saws before World War I. As already mentioned, Maine's continued prominence as a shipbuilding state was predicated on a constant supply of master carpenters and cheap local labor.[14] But Maine was not immune to national and international trends. As the nineteenth century wore on the aggregate number of shipbuilders in Maine decreased, and the remaining yards grew slightly larger.

An occasional attempt was made by Long Island shipbuilders to take advantage of the cost differential between Maine and Suffolk. In February of 1870, Nathaniel R. White of Northport contracted to build a 180-ton schooner for Captain James Velsor of Centerport. The ship was to be constructed at Calais, Maine. Unfortunately, a major fire on the Calais waterfront destroyed the schooner before it was finished.[15] It is not known whether or not White renewed the building. Similarly, in the same year, the Greenport partnership of Bishop and Ketcham prepared the model and moulds for a 200-ton schooner which was to be built at Bath, Maine.[16] Apparently, this particular foray into interstate shipbuilding was carried to a successful completion.

The shipbuilders blamed both foreign competition and high American tariffs for their increasing plight. On May 26, 1870, Henry A. Reeves, then representing the First Congressional District of New York in the Forty-first Congress, attacked a proposed bill that would have reduced the tariff on iron but not on copper. Reeves, who had three shipbuilding villages within his district, and who was a personal friend of James E. Bayles, had his speech featured prominently on the first page of the Greenport *Republican Watchman*. In his address to the House, Reeves claimed that the copper duty made American vessels $1500 more expensive than comparable ships constructed in Britain. In addition to the contracts lost because of higher American costs, vessels went abroad to be recoppered and American yards lost potential repair jobs. "Why admit iron of certain grades and exclude copper which is equally a necessity for the best class of ship?" Reeves asked. "If we want to promote shipbuilding so much that we are willing to repeal the [iron] tariff in its behalf, why not make the repeal effective by enabling the builders to get the best materials they need at the lowest possible rates?"[17] Reeves then charged the "American copper interests" with responsibility for the removal of copper from the bill's duty-free shipbuilding items. He went on to relate the reasons for his own struggle against the tariff.

"[I] have contented myself with steadily voting for a reduction of duties on all imports to the lowest possible standard consistent with a really economical administration of the federal government, believing that in doing so I was best fulfilling the measure of duty to my immediate constituency and to the people at large. Nor do I deem it well to depart from this course of conduct...did it not fall to my lot to represent the only district in the great state of New York, with her four million inhabitants and her ownership of over one-third of the total tonnage of the country, which is engaged to any considerable extent in the business of shipbuilding...Moreover there is perhaps no other district in the United States which furnished so large a quota of American seamen to the commercial marine, nor which contains so many people interested in maritime pursuits, proportional to its population, as does the first congressional district of New York.

"In the name of that industry now prostrate beneath the weight of adverse legislation and ruinous political policy, I undertake to say that shipbuilders do not ask for subsidies...[The] shipbuilders would simply say to the government, Do not cramp us in a match with our rivals across the big pond; do not protect other interests at our expense and we will gladly dispense with protection for ourselves.[18]"

Reeves then reiterated that he preferred a radical revision of the entire tariff code, but would accept the removal of certain items. Again he asked why lumber, timber, hemp, manila, composition metals and low grades of iron and steel could be removed, but not copper. He went on to voice another grievance of the shipbuilders and owners by asking Congress to "abolish the iniquitous and unbearable accumulation of charges for harbor master, quarantine, health officer and other special port fees and tonnage dues." He also asked for registration

The topsail schooner Fredericka Schepp, *built in 1879 as* Emma Ritch *by Jesse Carll, and active in the copra trade for the Schepp Cocoanut Company.*

fees for every foreign-built iron steam vessel over 2000 tons. Addressing the Republican administration, he concluded by combining his plea for the shipbuilders with another Democratic grievance:

"Cease your own fatal work of reconstructing the peaceful states; stop petting the freedmen of the South for political purposes and set them to growing the cotton, the tobacco, the sugar for which commerce will always find a ready market abroad and whose transportation will employ an amount of tonnage to which no man can fix a definite limit. Do these things and not only will American shipbuilding start at once into renewable activity, but that activity will continue and expand safely.[19]"

Reeves waxed eloquent on the subject of the copper industry, and it is likely he had been well coached by his friend James E. Bayles and possibly other shipbuilders as well. Unfortunately, his appeals, and their difficulties, proved less potent than the "American copper interests," and both copper and iron remained protected items. Later that year Reeves narrowly failed to be renominated for congressman, losing to Dwight Townsend of Queens County. Nevertheless, as noted earlier, Reeves remained an influential figure in Democratic party politics and his paper, the *Republican Watchman* continued as Suffolk's leading Democratic organ.

Complaints that the tariff was harming American shipbuilding were not confined to Henry Reeves or the 1870s. In November of 1880, the Port Jefferson *Times,* while reporting the construction of a steamer at Greenpoint (Brooklyn), commented, "We trust there will soon be such a revision of the tariff, that an impetus will be given to shipbuilding." Such was not to be. The protests from the shipbuilding community did not result in the abolition, or even reduction, of the tariffs on iron and copper. Not only were American metal producers exerting countervailing political pressure, but American shipping concerns were generally unsupportive. While the shippers sometimes claimed to be willing to purchase vessels built in America if these were price-competitive with British products, their bottom line was that they wanted the cheapest ships available. As early as 1869, the cheapest vessels were the long-lasting, metal-hulled ships turned out by the shipyards of the United Kingdom.[20]

The compulsory pilot fee charged in New York harbor was especially infuriating to the Suffolk shipbuilders. Their animus stemmed from a general dislike of anything that encumbered maritime trade and, undoubtedly, from their personal ownership of vessels whose profitability was reduced by such taxation. Agitation for removal of the fees reached a peak in 1880 when legislation was introduced in both Washington and Albany to remove the compulsory pilot fee. During this time James E. Bayles was in correspondence with an unknown party who was representing Queens County interests against the laws and wished to represent Suffolk as well. Bayles related the fragile state of Port Jefferson shipping, which he clearly ascribed, at least partly, to the costs of the pilot law. "We have in Port Jefferson," he wrote, "about 400 vessels enrolled with a tonnage of 20,000 tons or more, which, for the past two years have barely paid their own way and some not even that."[21]

In March of 1880, Bayles testified before the Congressional Committee of Commerce and Navigation and urged the repeal of the pilot fees. Here he was joined by his Setauket compatriot, Nehemiah Hand. Hand had already testified against pilot fees at a New York State Committee hearing where he closed his argument with a characteristically strong statement:

"Now gentlemen, this is our case exactly. We are compelled by law to pay for something we don't have and don't want. It is a robbery and a fraud. It is contrary to our republican form of government. It is contrary to our free institutions. It is a disgrace to our law-makers. It is a blot and stain on our statute books. It is the last relic of barbarism. Repeal this compulsory pilotage. Give us equal justice—this is all we want.[22]"

At the Congressional hearing Hand contented himself with submitting the pilot fees from Maine to Texas, demonstrating that New York rates were the highest. The shipbuilders and owners scored a partial success. Coasting vessels were no longer compelled to use pilots at Sandy Hook and Hell Gate. Hand went on record declaring that he would fight any compulsory pilotage as long as he lived.[23]

The advantage of cheap labor which allowed regional shipbuilding centers such as Long Island to continue after the Civil War could not stem the inexorable tide of change in the maritime economy. Although several of the yards in Northport and Port Jefferson enjoyed some prosperity in the 1866-1885 period, after 1885 the trade declined steadily with fewer yards, fewer workers and dwindling contracts. In this regard the Suffolk shipyards simply reflected the national trend. The 1900 Census of Manufacturers chronicles the degradation of wooden shipbuilding into small-boat construction. This census is especially revealing as it contrasts shipbuilding in 1900 with the situation ten years previous. In the number of establishments involved in wooden shipbuilding, 1900 posted a gain over 1890—1072 to 988. However, this was less impressive than it appeared since the census included spar, mast, boat and oar makers as "wooden shipbuilders." Even in this amorphous grouping the number of salaried men in the shipyards decreased 44.2 percent from 1890 and their salaries declined 34 per cent. There was a small increase of 1.4 percent in wage earners and a concomitant increase in wages.[24] Significantly, the number of vessels increased 54.4 percent while the value of the vessels declined $2,632,178, or 20.4 percent, "showing that the use of wood in shipbuilding is being restricted to smaller vessels than formerly."[25] The 1900 reports also demonstrate that the law of diminishing returns was operating in wooden ship and boat construction. Maine, for example, witnessed an increase of 36 firms engaged in "shipbuilding" between 1890 and 1900. This resulted in an increase in invested capital of $288,004 (28 per-

	Number	Gross Tons	Value
Steam launches	45	248	56,975
Power launches	552		54,643
Sailboats (under 5 tons)	332		74,189
Rowboats	1,756		125,870

Source: United States Census of Manufacturers, 1900, Vol. X, 214.

TABLE 6-1

Non-Military Vessels Constructed in New York State, 1900

	Number Estabs.	Proprietors Capital	Members	Avg. No. Workers	Total Wages
Metal	44	59,836,566	16	30,906	16,231,311
Wood	1,072	17,523,146	1,239	15,875	8,107,862

Source: United States Census of Manufacturers, 1900, Vol.X, 214

TABLE 6-1A

cent). Nevertheless, the value of products fell by $326,800 (11.6 percent) from the previous decade.[26]

In 1900 New York State contained the greatest number of shipbuilding establishments in the nation. This figure included metal shipyards and government facilities which were included in the census without differentiation. The New York State figures, which also included shipyards along the Hudson and on Lakes Ontario and Erie, also show an obvious shift from ship to boat construction. The 1900 Census also underscored the massive predominance of iron and steel over wood. Again, government yards were not indexed separately.

Additionally, the value of metal-hulled ships exceeded wooden vessels $50,367,739 to $24,210.419.[27] A comparison of the number of establishments, firm members and workers clearly shows the small-scale, almost primitive nature of the wooden shipbuilding concerns in relation to those engaged in iron and steel construction.

Metal's seizure of heavy shipbuilding from wood caused a southward shift from the traditional geographic centers of shipbuilding. While New York retained the largest gross number of shipbuilding establishments, it was second to Pennsylvania in total value of its products. Virginia, which had been a nonentity in shipbuilding during the previous decades of the century, rose to third place, primarily due to naval construction at Newport News and Norfolk.[28] The newly emerging pattern led Alexander R. Smith, author of the 1900 report on shipbuilding, to comment, "It is probably that the contest for shipbuilding in the next decade will be between the Delaware River and Chesapeake Bay District."[29]

An analysis of production figures from Port Jefferson shows the shift toward fewer and smaller vessels in Suffolk County. Though the statistics seem to indicate a resurgence of activity in 1901, this was not the case in terms of size and

	No.	Tonnage
Pre-1840	67	2,298 (incomplete)
1841-45	13	1,304 (incomplete)
1846-50	29	5,386 (incomplete)
1851-55	50	10,031
1856-60	17	5,670
1861-65	20	3,787
1866-70	23	4,182
1871-75	38	6,771
1876-80	20	2,866
1881-85	16	5,012
1886-90	8	1,772
1891-95	5	248
1896-1900	5	519
1901-05	14	2,492
1906-10	15	931
1910-17	4	small launches no tonnage reported

Source: Albert G. Hallock in Welles and Prios, 79-81.

TABLE 6-2
Vessels Reported Constructed at Port Jefferson, 1840-1917

The yacht Josephine, *built by Erastus Hartt and Oliver Hartt in about 1894.*

tonnage. Forty of the post-1891 vessels were motor launches, power yachts, commercial steam vessels and dredges. These were generally small—boats rather than ships—and required small crews. They were frequently expensive, however, some going as high as $75,000.[30] Though not as profitable as schooners and brigs, these smaller pleasure craft provided reasonable, if diminished, income for those with the skills to build and repair them. The 2492 tonnage figure for 1901-05 is an anomaly since almost half the number derived from the 1108-ton schooner *Martha E. Wallace.* Nevertheless, with income from the shipyards declining, those builders with other assets found the arguments for closing their yards increasingly persuasive. Of the original shipyards, only James E. Bayles held on until the First World War. He sold his operation in 1917, and it did not long survive under new owners. Indeed the construction of a traditional wooden ship had become something of a novelty after 1890. The last sizable vessel launched in Port Jefferson was the 1108-ton *Martha E. Wallace* built by John T. Mather and Owen E. Wood. As befitting the last of her breed, this coasting schooner was the largest sailing vessel ever built in Port Jefferson.

The watershed year for Long Island shipbuilding seems to have been 1885. The May 22 edition of the *Long Islander* for that year contained an overview of Northport's shipbuilding. Three yards were described as still in operation—Carll, Lefferts and Jarvis. They were described as the "most important department of manufacturing industry in our village...[and] at present are doing a thriving business."[31] William Mills, the village's chief sailmaker, was reported as having "so much work on hand that he is obliged to work day and night."[32] Apparently such hours did not appeal to Mills, for three months later he imported "a couple of New York sailmakers to help him." Despite Mills' reported activity it is interesting to note that he had already taken steps to diversify. This same issue which reported the booming sailmaking industry included a jarring note—the removal of Jesse Jarvis' "ways," signifying the end of one of the village's oldest shipyards. Nor did 1885 end on a happy note. The October 10 issue of the *Long Islander* warned that "work for ship carpenters during the coming winter promises to be slack."[33]

Northport was not alone in suffering from "slack" shipbuilding. On January 13, 1887, the Long Island *Leader* (Port Jefferson) published an article highly revealing of the state of shipbuilding and its wage scale. "The hum of labor again falls pleasantly on the ear. The long respite, enforced by the scarcity of work, has induced the eagerness for toil which the very low wages can not wholly abate."[34] Things did not look much better two years later. When Jesse Carll prepared to lay down a sand and brick schooner, the *Long Islander* remarked that "This news will be hailed with welcome by our ship carpenters who are anxious to see work in their line of work pick up."[35] Another sign of the changing times was the topic chosen by Port Jefferson Union School's 1893 valedictorian. The speaker, William E. Dayton, chose to discourse on the

The Mather shipyard early in the 20th century, with John McDermott *on the ways for repair and* Martha E. Wallace *under construction at left.*

"Decline of American Sailing Vessels." The address was printed in full in the August 8 Port Jefferson *Echo.* Young Dayton saw steam power, rail, road expansion and fierce competition among freight brokers causing the decline of America's maritime industries. Dayton stoically ascribed all of it to progress.

Progress it might have been but it was not without cost. With Jarvis folding up, Northport had three active shipbuilders: Jesse Carll, Edward Lefferts and Erastus Hartt. Hartt did not have a yard of his own and worked out of space in Carll's when he had a contract. In Port Jefferson the shipbuilders fell by the wayside rapidly. Sylvester T. Wines ceased production as early as 1869, Joseph J. Harris in 1878, Emmet Darling, the last of his family in the trade, threw in the sponge in 1880. Of the three builders still left in 1890 two, John Titus Mather and James E. Bayles, were descendants of the earliest of Port Jefferson's shipbuilding families.

The diminished shipbuilding community had two ways in which they could try to ward off extinction. One was to try to expand their repair work, the other was to try to adopt the new steam technology and produce more pleasure craft, both steam yachts and sailing yachts As has already been demonstrated (see Table 6-2, page 113), the bulk of Port Jefferson's post-1891 vessels were in exactly such a category. Although both James E. Bayles and John T. Mather produced steam launches and steam yachts, Mather and his ship designer Owen Wood were considered more expert in harnessing the new technology. They had considerable success building steam, sail and pleasure craft, which, along with steady repair work, induced them to install new steam railways with a 2500-ton capacity. In 1900 they established their own lumber yard with a steam saw and planing mill.[36]

The attempted transition to steam-powered vessels was partially abetted by the appearance of large-scale commercial oystering firms, which required steamers and dredges to harvest the abundant shellfish beds along the coasts and in the bays of Long Island. The Suwasset Oyster Company, formed in 1890, contracted with Long Island firms, most notably Mather and Wood, for several of its dredges. One year later Dexter Cole arrived in Northport from Connecticut to establish an oyster business. Huntington Town law prohibited all but local residents from harvesting bivalves in Town waters. Cole, who married a daughter of Jesse Carll, became one of the "Oyster Barons" whose homes were suitably situated along Northport's Bayview Avenue. His operations were later amalgamated with the Sealshipt system and Cole ran their Northport office until 1914. Cole and other oystermen placed orders for oyster steamers with the Northport yards. Cole designed the steamer *Supervisor* himself while his father-in-law did the construction.

Shipbuilding's decline was cushioned to some degree by the persistence, and possibly the increase, of repair work. Not that this was new. Shipbuilders had always repaired vessels as well as built them. Indeed, looking back on the late 1840s, Nehemiah Hand recalled he had "...all the repairing I could do."[37] By the 1880s, with new ship construction falling off, repair work must have taken on additional significance. Such work was certainly remunerative. The bill for a vessel named *John Breeze,* which was repaired by James M. Bayles in 1869, totalled $3428.08. Bayles netted $3139 for himself with the remainder going to Reuben H. Wilson (sails), Darling and Mather (lumber), E.F. Darling (chandlery), J.M. and G.F. Bayles (chandlery), and E. Hart and Sons (blacksmiths).[38] The list of subcontractors not only suggests the importance of the industry to the village but exposes the extent of diversification and interrelationships among the builders themselves. Bayles had one additional source of revenue from the vessel. He owned one-sixth of it. In New England yards, labor received more for repair work than for new construction, although it is not clear whether the Suffolk shipyards followed this practice.

Throughout the 1880s and 1890s, reports of repair work, its volume and pace, were scattered through Port Jefferson newspapers. Several of these notices

Oyster steamer Edna Chase *being launched in 1901 by the Hartts.*

Power yacht Alma *being built at the James E. Bayles yard in 1906.*

The oyster steamer Supervisor, *built by Jesse Carll in 1906 during the last years of wooden shipbuilding on Long Island.*

demonstrate the willingness of the builders to adjust to changed maritime conditions. Oyster steamers and steam yachts figure heavily in the repair items.[39] In 1885, the Babylon *Budget* reported that the Bayles yard "...always made a great specialty of repairing and overhauling yachts, probably more so than any other firm in the U.S. except in the large cities."[40]

Bayles does seem to have been the builder reaping the greater share of Long Island's rebuilding and repair business. In the fall of 1880, with new work on a three-masted schooner and a steam yacht in progress, Bayles was also engaged in rebuilding a sloop yacht, redoing the second deck on a Maine bark and carrying out "extensive" repairs to a Maine brig.[41] As the Port Jefferson *Watchman* noted: "...work has been pressing all the season, and at times not workmen enough could be got to do the work at hand."[42] Three years later, a newspaper report on a petition to improve harbor facilities included this assessment of the condition of the shipyards:

"At present the building of sailing vessels is somewhat dull, but the work of rebuilding and repairing is actively carried on and this gives occupation to many laborers and brings large sums of money to the place...There are some forty to fifty yachts which are either in the habit of repairing or wintering here.[43]"

The potential value of repair work to the builders may be partly glimpsed in the Manufacturing Censuses of 1860 and 1870. The absence of Port Jefferson and Setauket builders in the 1860 census makes complete evaluations impossible. The antebellum shipbuilding boom had collapsed by 1857, and this

	1860		1870	
	New Work	Repairs	New Work	Repairs
Jesse Jarvis	$2,000	$8,000	$10,000	$1,000
S.P. Hartt		8,000		
J.Carll		50,000	22,000	12,000
N. Hand			45,000	
E.M. Darling			7,500	
J.M. Bayles			22,000	3,000
C.L. Bayles			22,000	3,000
S. Wines			39,000	11,000
J.J. Harris			30,000	

Source: U.S. Census of Manufacturing, 1860,1870.

TABLE 6-3

Value of Repairs and New Work Reported in 1860 and 1870

clearly affected the Northport builders. Indeed, without repair work they would obviously have been in financial distress. In 1870, shipbuilding had made a partial recovery in some peripheral areas, including Suffolk County. All the builders reported making more from new construction than repair work. Nevertheless, repair work remained an important activity in their yards. Repairs amounted to better than one-sixth of the income of the Bayles brothers and more than one-half of Jesse Carll's earnings. By 1880, with new construction declining steadily, repairs became even more important.

Although the income derived from overhauling in this period is not known, the volume of repairs may be traced through newspapers. Comparisons of the amount of repairs with the production of new ships provides a good indication of the relative importance of the two activities to the shipbuilders (Tables 6-4, 6-5 and 6-6, page 120).

The figures in Table 6-4 demonstrate that in the early 1870s new construction still outranked repair work for J.M. Bayles, though two of his competitors were more dependent on repairs. Bayles built more vessels than he repaired in 1870-72, while Joseph J. Harris' ratio of repairs to construction was two to one. The figure of 152 vessels reported repaired by Jesse Carll during the two-year period is astounding and not entirely credible.[44] However, even if the number were exaggerated by half the real figure would be many times the five new vessels he launched. Table 6-5 provides a more precise breakdown of Northport builders and probably more accurate figures. The number of new vessels built in the yards is provided for comparison. Table 6-5 applies the same analysis to Port Jefferson builders a few years later. The large unknown figure most certainly

Port Jefferson	Repaired	Built
Bayles, J.M.	4	9
Harris, J.J.	4	2
Wines, S.	2	
Northport		
Carll, Jesse	152	5
Lefferts, E.	1	

Source: *Republican Watchman*, Feb. 3, 1872, BCH; Welles and Prios

Port Jefferson	Repaired	Built
Bayles, J.E.	16	1
Harris, J.J.	3	
Hawkins	2	
Mather & Wood	3	
Unknown	37	

Source:Port Jefferson *Times,* Port Jefferson *Echo*

Northport	Repaired	Built
Carll, Jesse	28	1
Lefferts, E/G	11	
Jarvis, J.	1	1
Hartt, E/O		1

Source: *Long Islander*

TABLE 6-4
Vessels Repaired and Built by Suffolk Builders, 1870-1872

TABLE 6-5
Vessels Repaired and Built by Suffolk Builders, 1888-1893

Port Jefferson	Repaired	Built
Bayles, J.E.	7	6
Mather & Wood	12	3
Hawkins	14	
Unknown	2	

Source: Port Jefferson *Echo*

Northport	Repaired	Built
Carll, Jesse	19	
Lefferts,E/G	8	
Hartt, E/O		1
Unknown		1

Source: *Republican Watchman, Long Islander*

TABLE 6-6
Vessels Repaired and Built by Suffolk Builders, 1900-1913

includes many vessels actually repaired by Bayles. The last table examines new construction and repair in Northport and Port Jefferson when the industry was in full retreat. The fall in Northport repairs was noticeable from the 1888-89 figures but, on the face of it, not as catastrophic as might have been predicted. Curiously, recorded information shows a greater deterioration in Port Jefferson. The largest number of repairs were carried out in the Hawkins yard, where no ships are known to have been constructed. The smaller number of vessels repaired by Bayles or Mather and Wood compared to work done by Carll at Northport was certainly offset by some new ship construction.

The fact that all the major builders were either out of the business or barely producing anything by World War I indicates that repair work was insufficient to keep the shipyards going. Repair work did not require the large gangs of men that new building demanded and was likely sporadic as well. Having evolved with the demand for wooden ships, Suffolk's shipyards were simply too big, perhaps too expensive, to maintain. Repairs, even when expanded to the increasing fleets of yachts on Long Island, could only slow the process of extinction.

The transition to steam vessels, especially large ones, may simply have been beyond the abilities of Long Island's shipyard owners, while repairs could not keep them afloat indefinitely. Both the founders and their sons, who came into their own as managers by the 1880s, had learned their craft in the halcyon age of wood and sail. Charles Thorn, who married a niece of James E. Bayles, believed the demise of the Bayles yard was partly due to his uncle's shortcomings. "Socially rather skillful he was a business getter but not a close bargainer," Thorn recalled. "The quality of the work commanded wide respect but he failed to maintain his plant adequately to the development of the industry and so enable it to get new business."[45] Unable to meet the demand for steel vessels during World War I, Bayles sold the yard to William B. Ferguson and John B. Smiley of the Smiley Steel Corporation in 1917. Ferguson and Smiley received a loan of a quarter-million dollars from the United States Shipping Board Emergency Fleet Corporation to renovate the yard for the production of steel-

The genial James E. Bayles is shown aboard one of his vessels in about 1900, accompanied by Captain Marshall.

hulled ships. The Emergency Fleet Corporation also bought the old Mather and Wood and John Hawkins yards. All three facilities were consolidated into a single unified operation under the Bayles name but without Bayles family participation. This stroke ended 100 years of independent shipbuilding in Port Jefferson.

Though the Bayleses were gone from shipbuilding, they were not forgotten. Their name was considered to have useful public-relations value and the new shipbuilding operation was dubbed the "Bayles Shipyard." Indeed, a promotional newsletter, the "Bayles Booster," declared that "...the Bayles Shipyard will be the great contributing factor to the greater prosperity and advancement of good old Port Jefferson."[46] And so it seemed—for a while. Between November of 1917 and January of 1919, the workforce mushroomed from 250 to 1100 workers, with a weekly payroll of over $30,000.[47] The 20 ships from the North Atlantic Fleet stationed near the village also contributed to the heady, but artificial, wartime boom. The "Bayles Shipyard" did not long survive the war. It closed its gates in 1920 and Port Jefferson's "greater prosperity" disappeared overnight.

Despite an investment of $7,000,000 during the 1917-20 period,[48] the output of the Emergency Fleet Corporation shipyard was unimpressive. Two seagoing tugs, the first steel-hulled vessels built in Port Jefferson, were launched in 1919. They were followed by two freighters and two scows, according to one record. Another record lists three freighters of 5000 tons each and a tanker measured at 1200 tons. The low productivity was caused to some degree by local

Vessels at the huge new Bayles Shipyard during World War I.

The Bayles Shipyard during World War I with steel vessels in progress.

workers' lack of experience with steel ships as well as waste and inefficiency on the part of the Emergency Fleet Corporation. The career of the "Bayles Shipyard" indicates that Port Jefferson and its wooden-ship-trained workforce was not suited to metal construction. This conclusion was reached by at least some contemporary observers. In March of 1920, the Brooklyn *Eagle* attacked the enterprise, questioning the attempt to run a modern shipbuilding operation so far from workers skilled in steel techniques and readier access to raw materials.[49] The *Eagle* was probably right, but the Brooklynites may also have been annoyed that yards closer to home did not receive the contracts.

In 1920 the "Bayles Shipyard" was sold to the New York Harbor and Drydock Company, which completed the ships that remained partly built and then broke up the operation into the original separate yards and sold them individually. Yard No. 2, the old Mather yard, was taken over by the Bridgeport and Port Jefferson Steamship Company which has run a ferry service from the site ever since. The Hawkins yard eventually became a Long Island Lighting Company facility. Although some attempt was made to use the Bayles yard for yacht repair and outfitting, the wartime renovations made this impossible. Shipbuilding was not to be revived in Port Jefferson.

In Northport, the decline of shipbuilding paralleled the experience of Port Jefferson with less of a cushion from pleasure-boat construction. Jesse Carll died in 1902 and his son Jesse, Jr., who had been managing the firm, assumed total control. The yard struggled on, primarily through repair work, its economic health deteriorating. The First World War provided some lift, though on a much smaller scale than at Port Jefferson. Carll leased his ways to a firm which had a contract to build scows for the navy. Two were completed and a third under construction when the war ended. All work ceased immediately. The yard reverted to Carll who abandoned the business entirely, donating the site to Northport as a park. Traditional shipbuilding on Long Island had passed into history.

Notes:

1.   U.S. Congress, House, *Report of the Select Committee on the Causes of the Reduction of American Tonnage* (House of Representatives, 28 41st Congress, 2nd Session. 1870. Hereafter cited as the Lynch Report, 30.

2.   Robert G. Albion, "Foreign Trade in the Era of Wooden Ships" in *The Growth of the American Economy,* ed. by Harold F. Williamson (Englewood Cliffs: Prentice-Hall, 1957), 225.

3.   *Republican Watchman,* December 25, 1869, 1.

4.   United States Department of Commerce, Bureau of the Census, Twelfth Census of the United States, 1900. Volume X, Manufacturers. Part IV, *Shipbuilding* by Alexander R. Smith, 209.

5.   Lynch Report, 91. See also Pollard, Sydney and Robertson, Paul. *The British Shipbuilding Industry, 1870-1914* (Cambridge, Mass: Harvard University Press), 11.

6.   C.K. Hartley, "On the Persistence of Old Techniques, *The Case of North American Wooden Shipbuilding.*" Journal of Economic History, XXXIII, No. 2, 1973, 377.

7.   Lynch Report, 85.

8.   Ibid., 31.

9.   Ibid., 91.

10.   Ibid., 11, 19.

11.   Hartley, 381.

12.   Hutchins, John G.B., *The American Maritime Industries and Public Policy, 1789-1914* (Cambridge, Mass: Harvard University Press, 1941), 76.

13.   Ibid., 543.

14.   Ibid., 560.

15.   *Republican Watchman,* September 17, 1870, 3.

16.   Ibid., August 13, 1870, 3.

17.   RW, June 4, 1870, 1.

18.   Ibid.

19.   Ibid.

20. Lynch Report, 1 and passim.

21. James E. Bayles, undated letter, c.1880. Frances Child Collection.

22. Richard M. Bayles, "Brookhaven" in *Munsell's History of Suffolk County* (New York: W.W. Munsell and Co., 1882), 86.

23. Ibid.

24. Smith, 210.

25. Ibid.

26. Smith, 214.

27. Ibid.

28. Smith, 216.

29. Ibid., 218.

30. *Long Islander,* Oct. 5, 1911, 3.

31. *Long Islander,* May 22, 1885, 5.

32. Ibid., May 15, 1885, 3.

33. Ibid., October 10, 1885, 3.

34. Long Island *Leader,* January 13, 1887, cited in Welles and Prios, 31.

35. *Long Islander,* February 2, 1889, 2.

36. Welles and Prios, 41-42.

37. *Munsell's History of Suffolk County* (New York: W.W. Munsell and Co., 1883), 85.

38. Mss. Frank & Frances Child Collection

39. Port Jefferson *Times,* October 14, 1883, *Long Islander,* May 1, 1885, Port Jefferson *Watchman,* September 7, 1889.

40. Babylon *Budget,* February 21, 1885, 2.

41. Port Jefferson *Watchman,* September 7, 1889, 2.

42. Ibid.

43. Port Jefferson *Times,* May 20, 1892, 4.

44. Republican *Watchman,* February 3, 1872, 4.

45. James M. Bayles, *Well-Worn Ways,* typescript. c.1950, FFCC.

46. Welles and Prios, 61.

47. Ibid.

48. Welles and Prios, 62.

49. Ibid., 24.

CHAPTER SEVEN

Aftermath

The men who had led Suffolk County's rise as a provincial shipbuilding center did not long survive its demise. Indeed, some of the pioneers died before the inexorable decline of their trade had run its course. Nathaniel R. White, a Northport builder of modest output but a lengthy career, blazed a path for subsequent generations of Long Islanders by retiring to Florida, where he died February 20, 1885. The first of the "giants" to pass away was James M. Bayles who died March 29, 1889. On April 1, the day of his funeral, flags flew at half mast on all the ships in the harbor as well as on Port Jefferson's public buildings. The remaining major shipbuilders, including Jesse Carll, attended the rites which boasted a consortium of Baptist, Presbyterian and Methodist ministers. The Port Jefferson *Times* editorialized that "while his shipbuilding enterprise may have been of great pecuniary advantage to himself, it also was of considerable benefit to Port Jefferson—more so than any other single business enterprise here."[1] Three years later the Floral Park *Times* delivered its own encomium, making the comment that "The firm of James M. Bayles and Son, more than any other, perhaps, have by their conscientious workmanship and handsome modelling rendered Brookhaven vessels famous for their speed, carrying capacity and fine outline."[2]

The next major builder to die was Jesse Carll. As early as 1883 Carll was described as having an "active, nervous temperament that works on the high pressure principle often making a physical and mental slave of its possessor."[3] The same account records his having suffered two near-breakdowns, which necessitated vacations in Mexico and Canada. He also began to rely more heavily on Jesse, Jr., in operating the business. Carll's situation never seems to have gotten much better and newspaper notices in his later years report many trips away from Northport in an attempt to restore his health. In his later years Carll predicted the collapse of shipbuilding except for the repair of yachts for the wealthy.[4] The end finally came in October, 1902. The shipbuilder, whose wealth was estimated at $250,000, was buried in a mahogany coffin. All businesses in Northport were closed on October 27, the day of the funeral. Flags stood at half mast both on shore and on vessels in the harbor.[5]

The last of Port Jefferson's great shipbuilders, John T. Mather and James E. Bayles, died in 1928 and 1929 respectively. Mather, who had finally sold out his yards to oysterman Quaker Randal before World War I, died March 30, 1928, while visiting Havana. The family home on Prospect Street, now the headquarters of the Port Jefferson Historical Society, was left to his cousin, Florence

Smith. His financial estate totalled $1,820,917.72.[6] Mather gave the bulk of the estate—$1,433,439.70—for the construction and outfitting of a hospital, now Mather Memorial. The remainder was allocated to trust funds. Any amount left after their extinction was to be placed in an endowment fund for the hospital. James E. Bayles died in March, 1929. Published reports stated that he left an estate "formally valued at over $10,000." Actually, his bequests, excluding real-estate holdings, came to under $9000. His real estate, which seems confined to his house, was also valued at $9000.[7] Bayles' private library of 1212 volumes, manuscripts, journals and log books devoted to nautical subjects was bequeathed to his niece, Charlotte, who promptly dispersed it. The enormous disparity between the estates of these two highly successful shipbuilders is not readily explicable. It may be that Mather's other economic interests were more profitable and possibly he lived more frugally as well. Neither Mather nor Bayles were honored with a display of flags at half mast in the harbor. By 1928 such a gesture would have seemed anachronistic.

There is some evidence that nineteenth-century shipbuilders were aware of the impending fate of their industry and took steps to direct their children into other fields—and frequently out of Suffolk County. While Jesse Carll's eldest son, Jesse, Jr., continued to manage the family shipyard until its demise, another son, Benjamin, moved to Brooklyn. Carll saw one of his daughters marry into the Commack Burrs, a financial and real-estate power in Suffolk, and another married oysterman Dexter Cole. From this last line descends the Seymour family which operates the Seymour boatyard, a repair and boat-storage operation located a little north of the old Carll yard.

James E. Bayles' only son, Stephen Taber Bayles, predeceased him in 1919. Although he had worked for a time with his father, the junior Bayles left Port Jefferson as a young man and moved to New York City. Here he joined the banking firm of Gilman and Son. He remained with them for 25 years before joining the Norden Trust Company. Failing health forced him to retire in 1912, when he returned to Port Jefferson.[8] The male line of the Bayleses suffered further loss with the death of George F. Bayles, Jr., whose father ran the family store. Hamilton T. Bayles, George's brother, worked at the store but left to work at the government-financed "Bayles Shipyard" during World War I. Before his death in 1922, Hamilton Bayles served on the Town Board of Trustees, was treasurer of the Port Jefferson Fire Department and Cedar Hill Cemetery, and was chairman of the Board of Education. Another brother, Samuel, was still involved with the "Bayles Shipyard" in 1922. John T. Mather left no issue and there are no direct male descendants bearing either the Mather or Bayles name on Long Island today.

Most of the other families engaged in Long Island shipbuilding left even less of a trace. George Hand, who had inherited Setauket's most important yard, folded the business by 1893. In that year he secured the position of Inspector of

Hulls at the New York Custom House. He was the first Suffolk man to receive an appointment from Grover Cleveland.[9]

The R.H. Wilson sail loft provides a good illustration of how one trade adapted to shifting situations. Reuben H. Wilson, the company's founder, died in 1876. His sons, Frederick and Advance, inherited the company. When Frederick died in 1904 his son, Richard N., took over. In 1932 Richard recounted the measures taken by the Wilsons to stay afloat:

"When we realized that sails were things of the past, we then gave up sail-making; even our employees who had been with us for years, and these were among the best sailmakers in the world, were replaced by people trained especially for awning work.

"We found we must change with the times, but we always try to keep ahead of our line. We are still doing business with one or two firms as old or a little older than we are, but in looking over our books, we find most of the large concerns we used to do business with have passed out. Even their names are unknown to the present generation.

"We can't help feeling proud that we are still going, old in experience, but young as we were ninety years ago when it comes to difficult rush jobs.[10]"

The Wilsons do not seem to have troubled themselves about the fate of the veteran sailmakers they turned out when they tacked about to meet the winds of change. As Richard tells the story, the Wilsons were quite cold-hearted in their economic decisions. It must be remembered, however, that he was not a major participant in the transition he describes. His father might have found making such decisions much harder than Richard does in retelling them. Yet such hard-edged realism might have been the only way to look at things in the depths of the Depression. Perhaps it was this steely attitude that Charles Thorn, son-in-law of James E. Bayles, had in mind when he wrote that his father-in-law lacked the gift of being a "close bargainer." For the Wilsons, the transition from sails to awnings was not enormous. It might be said to have been a natural extension of a skill. For the shipbuilders no such evolution was possible. The collapse of the American merchant marine, excepting the unnatural 1917-19 spurt, left nothing but repairs and the occasional yacht contract. These were no longer enough to carry enterprises of such scale.

The era of Long Island shipbuilding, which had been such an important feature of the region's economic life for most of a century, passed with remarkable suddenness. By the mid-1920s hardly a trace of the shipyards could be detected in any of the former shipyard villages. The labor force had long since scattered, the number of survivors declining yearly as new generations grew to maturity with little inkling of the Island's shipbuilding traditions. The great shipbuilding families had abandoned the trade, dispersed, and lost the pre-eminence they once held in local social and economic life. Except for the very old with their memories, by the middle of the twentieth century Long Island shipbuilding was of interest primarily to antiquarians.

Shipbuilding on Long Island was a regional manifestation of a major national enterprise. When the larger forces which drove the demand for wooden sailing ships subsided, and American maritime activity began to fade, so did the Island's shipyards. Suffolk County's shipbuilders were men of skill who constructed vessels well able to hold their own in both coasting and deepwater trades. Additionally, some of them were entrepreneurs of no mean ability. Before the era of American sail came to an end, the Long Island shipbuilders had enriched themselves, brought prosperity to their communities, and—in the middle decades of the nineteenth century at least—contributed to the affluence and economic development of their nation as well. What small fame human memory and local tradition still renders them was justly earned.

Notes:
1. Port Jefferson *Times*, April 3, 1889, 1.
2. Floral Park *Times*, quoted in Thorn, *Well Worn Ways*.
3. *Munsell's History of Suffolk County* (New York: W.W. Munsell and Co., 1882), 87-88.
4. Jesse Carll, IV, Recorded interview. No date c. 1978. Northport Public Library.
5. *Long Islander*, October 31, 1902, 1.
6. New York *Times*, —25, 1929, clipping from Frances Child Collection (month missing).
7. James E. Bayles, Administration Papers. Suffolk County Surrogate's Court, File 31032.
8. Brooklyn *Eagle*, January 18, 1919.
9. Port Jefferson *Echo*, March 29, 1893, 3.
10. *Suffolk Every Sunday*, February 10, 1932, 12.

The Number of Ships Built on Long Island

A totally accurate listing of all Long-Island-built ships has not yet been printed. The number constructed after 1855 has been approximated with some degree of accuracy, but statistics before that date are somewhat problematical. The basic source for Long Island-built ships is the shipbuilding appendix to the *Bi-Centennial History of Suffolk County*, printed in 1885. This is relied upon by almost all authorities. The value of the compilation is that the date, 1885, immediately precedes the decline of the industry on Long Island. While vessels were constructed long after 1885, their numbers are known to have fallen steeply. However, the *Bi-Centennial History's* compilers depended on information supplied by the builders who often had incomplete lists or were, perhaps, purposefully vague. The *History's* statistics are laid out in a manner that prevents a precise totaling of a given year's output. For example, the BCH lists Gideon Smith of Stony Brook as having built three schooners between 1835 and 1868. Obviously a minor builder, he may have been building a ship in 1840, thus warranting the inclusion of his vessel in that year's total, but he might just as easily have been idle that year.

Additionally, many builders, especially those outside of Port Jefferson, simply supplied lists of vessels with no attempt to arrange them in chronological order. Consequently, it is frequently impossible to determine the exact year in which a particular ship was built. This creates major difficulties in ascertaining the percentage of Suffolk-built ships in the New York State total. One hundred and one ships were reported constructed in New York State in the state census of 1855. Only 15 vessels, 15 percent of the total, are definitely known to have been built in Suffolk County that year. However, the large number of vessels unassigned to any set year suggests that Suffolk's share of the New York State total was considerably higher, probably closer to 25 percent. In 1865, with 39 vessels listed as built in New York according to the state census, Suffolk can be credited with nine, or 23 percent of them. Again, the large number of unchronologically assigned vessels suggests that this is an underestimate.

A much more exact breakdown of vessels constructed is found in Welles and Prios, *Port Jefferson, The Story of a Village*. These figures are more accurate and complete than the BCH as they include information gleaned from ship registrations and follow the industry to its vanishing point in 1917.

A different problem with ship statistics occurs in Henry Hall's highly useful and incisive *Shipbuilding Industry of the United States,* which was published as a special supplement to the 1880 Census. Interestingly, and confusingly, his statistics, reproduced in Table 1-5, page 19, do not paint as gloomy a picture as his narrative. Hall's narrative tells us that Port Jefferson builders constructed four ships in 1880, Greenport one, and that none were launched in Setauket or Northport. Since his tables list 18 vessels built in Suffolk, 13 vessels are left unclaimed. Several other Suffolk ports occasionally built ships, and the South Shore from Bay Shore to Patchogue constructed small, mostly cat-rigged, boats for finfishing and shellfishing in the Great South Bay. Indeed, Hall reports 17 such boats built in that area in 1880. Their low tonnage—five to 24 tons—makes them an unlikely source of much of the 147,750 tons reported built in 1880. However, if five ships were built on the North Shore in 1880 and 17 on the South, the total number of Suffolk vessels should be 22, not 18 as Hall lists them in his statistical tables.

The discrepancies in Hall's statistics, and a comparison of his statistics to his narrative, suggest that he may have excluded certain categories from either the tables or the text. Whatever his now-lost criteria may have been, the fact remains that he is not consistent. The most likely explanation is that he was more impressionistic in his narrative than his charts. To return to his listing of vessels built on the North Shore in 1880, his figures should be compared to the BCH and Welles and Prios. They claim five vessels built in Port Jefferson, two in Greenport and one in Northport.

Wooden Shipbuilders
in Suffolk County, New York, 1800-1900

* An asterisk indicates a major builder

Cold Spring Harbor:

Elwood Abrams	active 1868-1873
John Bennet	active 1866-1867
Daniel Gillies	active 1868
Robert Hubble	active c. 1860
John H. Jones	active c. 1850
Platt C. Place	active 1869
A. L. Rawlins	active 1846
Theodore Rowland	active 1845
N. Seaman	active c. 1845
William Sturdivant	active c. 1860
Henry Titus	active 1836
Alfred Van Cott	active 1848
John Dudley Velsor	active 1848
Abraham Waters	active c. 1860

Huntington Harbor:

Isaac Scudder Ketcham	active c. 1860
Charles Sammis	active c. 1860

Northport:

Bunce and Bayles	active 1828
C. Beebee	active 1812
David Carll	active 1855-1865
Jesse Carll *	1832-1902
Jesse Carll, Jr.	active 1880-1914
Moses Brush Hartt	1808-1875
Samuel Prior Hartt *	active 1803-1879
Erastus Hartt	1825-1913
Oliver Hartt	1848-1921
Jesse Jarvis *	1817-1898
Edwin Lefferts	1818 (?)-1906
Nathaniel R. White	died 1885

Stony Brook:

David T. Bayles	1825-1893
Samuel Carman	active c. 1850-1860

Jesse Davis	active c. 1850-1860
Richard Davis	active c. 1850-1860
William Davis	active c. 1850-1860
Ebenezer Hallock	active c. 1850-1860
Joel Raynor	active c. 1850-1860
Elias Smith	active c. 1850-1860
Gideon Smith	active c. 1850-1860
Jonas Smith	active c. 1850-1860
William Welles	active c. 1850-1860
Daniel T. Williamson	active c. 1850-1860

Setauket:

William Bacon	active 1846-1874
David B. Bayles	1808-1892
David Cleves	active 1820-1833
Nehemiah Hand *	1819-1895
George Hand	active 1876-1893
Brewster Hawkins	active 1825-1869

Patchogue:

O. Perry Smith	active 1850-1872

Port Jefferson:

Elisha Bayles	active c. 1812-1830
James M. Bayles *	1815-1889
C. Lloyd Bayles	active 1855-1874
James E. Bayles *	died 1929
S.F. Bird	1884
Edgar Brown	active c. 1830-1832
Benjamin Brown	active c. 1832-1851
Charles Darling	active c. 1851-1852
Emmet B. Darling	active c. 1870-1879
Jeremiah Darling	actice c. 1840-1867
John E. Darling	active 1844-1867
J.L. Darling	active 1852-1854
Mathew Darling	active 1842-1848
Henry Hallock	active 1855-1878
Silas Hand	1802-1875
Joseph J. Harris	active c. 1858-1878
Ahira Hawkins	active c. 1852-1860
Lewis Hulse	active c. 1832-1855
William L. Jones	1792-1860
William M. Jones	1821-1905
E. Ketcham	active 1856-1860

John Marion	1856
Richard Mather	1786-1816
John Richard Mather *	1814-1899
John Titus Mather *	1854-1928
Titus Mather	active c. 1824-1825
Isaac Rich	1839
Joseph Rowland	1852
L. M. Rowland	1861-1865
John E. Smith	1854
Sylvester Smith	active c. 1832-1846
Owen Wood	active c. 1880-1902

Greenport:

Richard Benjamin	active c. 1855-1865
Harmon D. Bishop	active c. 1850
Hiram Bishop	active c. 1839-1855
Oliver H. Bishop	active c. 1860-1882
Cornelius Ketcham	active c. 1860
Hiram Ketcham	active c. 1860-1880
Charles M. Smith	active c. 1867-1882

Bibliography

PRIMARY SOURCES

1. Manuscripts

A. Shipbuilding and Shipbuilders

Daniel B. Bayles Ledger, 1854-1857. Three Village Historical Society.

Frank & Frances Child Collection. (Bayles Family Archives).

Records of R.G. Dun and Company. Baker Library, Harvard Graduate School of Business Administration.

Contract, Samuel Prior Hartt with Captain William Hamilton and Samuel S. Brown. October 24, 1863. Huntington Historical Society.

Ledger, 1820-1847. Anonymous Shipbuilder-Merchant. Three Village Historical Society.

Norman O'Berry Collection. Local History Room. Smithtown Public Library.

Vessel Book. Sloop *Woodcock*, 1807-1810. Three Village Historical Society.

Daniel Y. Williamson Papers. Museums at Stony Brook.

B. Government Documents

Town of Brookhaven Tax Assessments, 1860-1890. Brookhaven Town Historian's Office.

Town of Huntington Tax Assessments, 1860-1884. Huntington Town Historian's Office. 1890, Town Assessor's Office.

United States Manuscript Censuses, 1850-1900.

United States Manufacturing Censuses, 1850, 1860, 1870. Administration Papers, James E. Bayles. Suffolk County Surrogate Court.

Will, Jesse Carll. June 7, 1902. Suffolk County Surrogate Court.

Will and Administration Papers, Nehemiah Hand. March 12, 1895. Suffolk County Surrogate Court.

2. Published Primary Sources

A. Government Documents

Census of the New York State for 1855. Albany: Charles Van Benthuysen, 1857.

Census of the State of New York for 1865. Albany: Charles Van Benthuysen, 1867.

Census of the State of New York for 1875. Albany: Weed, Parson and Company, 1877.

Sleight, Henry D. *Town Records of the Town of Smithtown,* 2 Vols. Smithtown, 1929.

Street, Charles R. (compiler) *Huntington Town Records,* 3 Vols. Huntington, 1889.

United States Congress, House, Report of the Select Committee on the Causes of the Decline of American Tonnage. House of Representatives, 28, 41st Congress. 2nd Session. "Lynch Report." Washington, DC: Government Printing Office, 1870.

United States Department of Commerce. Bureau of The Census, *United States Census of Population, 1880.* Vol. VIII. *The Shipbuilding Industry of the United States,* by Henry Hall. Washington, DC, 1884.

United States Department of Commerce, Bureau of the Census. *Twelfth Census of the United States, 1900.* Volume X. *Manufactures,* Part IV, "Shipbuilding," by Alexander R. Smith, Washington, DC.

B. Primary County and Area Materials

Bayles, Richard M. *Historical and Descriptive Sketches of Suffolk County,* Port Jefferson, 1874.

Bi-Centennial History of Suffolk County, Babylon: Budget Steam Print, 1885.

Boyd's Directory of Long Island, New York, 1864-65.

Munsell's History of Suffolk County, New York: W.W. Munsell and Company, 1883.

C. Newspapers

Long Islander (Huntington).

Port Jefferson *Times*.

Port Jefferson *Echo*.

Republican Watchman (Greenport).

SECONDARY SOURCES

1. Shipbuilding

Albion, Robert G. "Foreign Trade in the Era of Wooden Ships." *The Growth of the American Economy*, Edited by Harold F. Williamson. Englewood Cliffs: Prentice-Hall, 1957.

Bayles, James M. *Well Worn Ways*, A Brief History of the Bayles Shipyard on Long Island, Typescript, c.1960.

Goldenberg, Joseph A. *Shipbuilding in Colonial America*. Charlottesville, Va: University of Virginia Press, 1976.

Hartley, C.K. "On the Persistence of Old Techniques: The Case of North American Wooden Shipbuilding." Journal of Economic History, XXXIII, 2, (June, 1973), 372-98.

Hutchins, John G.B. *The American Maritime Industries and Public Policy*, 1789-1914. Cambridge, Mass: Harvard University Press, 1941.

Minuse, William, *Shipbuilding in Setauket*, Mimeographed. 1955.

Morrison, John H. *History of New York Shipyards*, Port Washington: Kennikat Press, 1970. (Reprint of 1909 Edition).

Pollard, Sidney and Robertson, Paul. *The British Shipbuilding Industry, 1870-1914*. Cambridge, Mass: Harvard University Press, 1979.

2. Regional, County, Town and Village History

Fletcher, William L. *Historic Greenpoint*, Greenpoint Savings Bank, 1919.

Gabriel, Ralph, *Evolution of Long Island*, 1921.

History of Huntington Township. Papers Read Before the Huntington Historical Society during the Season of 1918-1919, 1919-1920. Oakley Papers. Mss. Huntington Historical Society.

Johnston, Guy E. (compiler). *Detailed History and Description of the Original Township of Huntington, 1653-1800*, 1925-1930. North, 1926.

Ross, Peter. *History of Long Island*, 2 Vols. New York: Lewis Publishing Company, 1902.

Sammis, Ramonah. *History of the Town of Huntington*, Huntington: Huntington Historical Society, 1937.

Simpson, Richard and Wagner, Gay. *History of Bayview Avenue*. Mimeograph, Northport Historical Society, c.1970.

Stiles, Henry R. *History of the County of Kings and City of Brooklyn, New York:* W.W. Munsell and Company, 1884.

Gordon Welles and William Prios. *Port Jefferson, The Story of A Village*. Port Jefferson: Historical Society of Greater Port Jefferson, 1977.

3. Miscellaneous

Chandler, Alfred D. *The Visible Hand, The Managerial Revolution In American Business*. Cambridge, Mass: Harvard University Press, 1977.

North, Douglas C., Anderson, Terry L. and Hill, Peter J. *Growth and Welfare in the American Past. A New Economic History*. Englewood Cliffs: Prentice-Hall, 1983.

Thernstrom, Stephen. *Poverty and Progress, Social Mobility in a Nineteenth Century City*. New York: Antheneum, 1975.

Recorded Materials

Interview With Jesse Carll III. c.1976. Northport Public Library.

William Minuse. *Shipbuilding in Brookhaven*. Taped Lecture. March 21, 1975. Suffolk County Historical Society.

Index

Bold numerals indicate illustrations.

Velsor, James, 108

Wages, 83, 85, 86, 94, 95, 96, 114
Wealth, 57-67, 86, 87, 89, 90
White, Nathaniel R., 75, 108, 127
White oak, 8, 9, 29
Whitlock and Glover, 49
Wilkes-Barre (coal barge), 48
Williamson, Daniel Y., 40
Willse, Irene, 2
Willse, John, 2, 30, 31, 32, 33
Willse connection, 3
Wilson, Advance, 64, 129
Wilson, Frederick, 18, 75, 129
Wilson, Frederick M., 64, 73
Wilson, Reuben H., 64, 72, 129
Wilson, Richard N., 129
Wines, Sylvester, 39, 115
Wing, J. and W.R., 30
Wood, Owen, 30, 35, 114
Woodcarvers, 64
Woodcock (sloop), 49
Woodhouse and Rudd, 50, 62
Workforce, 13-14, 15, 16, 17, 18, 65,
        66, 91
Work habits, 26
Working conditions, 85

Yachts, 18, 114, 116, 118
Yellow pine, 8, 30

Illustration Credits

Dust-jacket photo: Mystic Seaport Museum
x   Frank and Frances Child Collection
xi   Port Jefferson Historical Society
4   Three Village Historical Society
5   Three Village Historical Society
6   Map courtesy of the author
7   Map courtesy of the author
         Pullout map from Benjamin F. Thompson's *History of Long Island*
         Mystic Seaport photo by Claire White-Peterson
10   Three Village Historical Society
26,   27, 28, 29 Engravings from *Harper's New Monthly Magazine* courtesy of the
         G.W. Blunt White Library, Mystic Seaport Museum
31,   32, 36, 37 Engravings from *Munsell's History of Suffolk County*
44   Northport Historical Society
46   Port Jefferson Historical Society
47   Mystic Seaport Museum
48   Mystic Seaport Museum
51   Frank and Frances Child Collection
65   William J. Mills II
72   Both photographs from the Frank and Frances Child Collection
77   Long Island Collection, The Queens Borough Public Library
78   Mystic Seaport Museum
84   Port Jefferson Historical Society
97,   98, 99, 100, 101 Mystic Seaport Museum
107   The Society for the Preservation of New England Antiquities
109   Mystic Seaport Museum
113   Northport Historical Society
115   Port Jefferson Historical Society
117   Northport Historical Society (above), Mystic Seaport Museum (below)
118   Mystic Seaport Museum
121   Port Jefferson Historical Society
122,   123 Long Island Collection, The Queens Borough Public Library

Composed in Adobe Garamond
Designed by Barbara Rogan, Stonington Design, Mystic, Connecticut
Printed by Thomson-Shore, Dexter, Michigan